JUDGE RANDALL
AT THE LONG GONE

JUDGE RANDALL
AT THE LONG GONE

TONY ROGERS

A Judge Randall Prequel

Other titles in the Judge Randall series:

ISBN: 979-8-9864655-0-0 (Paperback)
ISBN: 979-8-9864655-1-7 (Ebook)

Published by Quinn Cove Books

Thanks again to Joan Seymour for her editorial help.

Cover Design by Berge Design

to Tamara

A note to the reader –

Judge Randall At The Long Gone is a courtroom drama with a thriller twist at the end. It takes place after Judge Randall retires from the Massachusetts Superior Court but before he begins his second career as an amateur detective. It is a prequel to the Judge Randall mysteries.

1

Ernie Farrell was a very bright man. He worked beneath his intelligence, but he was smart. Too smart for his own good, his father often said.

Ernie held his pickup steady as an eighteen-wheeler blew by on his left. He was driving distracted this morning. Too much on his mind. Janet, job, life in general. He had been thinking in recent days that maybe it was time he got serious. He had traded on potential for a long time. Perhaps it was time to put up or shut up.

He made a right turn, almost clipping a bicycle rider. Bike lanes were good in theory, problematic in practice. Traffic was bad this morning. Not that it was ever light. Permanent gridlock was on its way, and what would the country do then? Would offices be outlawed? Would telecommuting be mandatory for all?

He took the sharp left into his parking lot. His office was in a low stucco building that could easily pass for an auto repair shop, a plumbing supplier, or a derelict gas station, but in fact was home to one of the many startups clustered near MIT. Ernie worked for a small video game developer that so far had only one game, for which Ernie had written the code.

Ernie's cubicle was near the rear door. The other three software programmers were already hard at work. He nodded to them and got down to business.

Programming appealed to the fussbudget area of his cortex while allowing him to daydream. He could simultaneously write a string of code and imagine himself on his favorite mountain trail, rescuing an errant hiker who had fallen and broken a leg. He would improvise a stretcher out of his tent to slide the hiker down the slope to safety. He could smell the pines and the pungent soil, he could hear the hiker's plea. "Help me, please. I'm in terrible pain."

Ernie would calmly reply, "Don't worry, I'll get you down safely."

Time passed quickly while he was at work, and the long days seemed short. He left the office for home at 8 p.m.

Traffic was lighter than usual. One could never predict traffic, commutes you thought would be quick were endless, and vice versa. Maybe he would write a gambling app for major routes. Predict time and place where traffic would seize up. Earn money while gridlocked. Now that would be a big seller.

It was dark and his mind wandered. This evening it landed him in a kayak off the Maine coast, navigating the waves. The sea was heavy, but his arms were strong. He felt confident and full of life.

He was approaching the entrance to I-93 north. He texted Janet to tell her he'd be home soon, then moved into the right-hand lane. At the entrance he glanced in his rear view mirror to begin his turn. A flash of light and a screech of tires yanked him back to reality, followed by a thud unlike any he had heard before.

A driver somewhere behind him leaned on his horn. On the sidewalk, a woman waved her arms frantically, a look of horror on her face, and he realized the woman was signaling him.

He stopped his pickup and got out but wasn't prepared for what he saw: a mangled bike on the sidewalk and a shoeless foot sticking out from beneath his rear right wheel.

Time sped up after that. He found himself in a police car on the way to the station to give a statement. Then he found himself in Janet's car, and she was driving him home. Everything he said at the police station was a blur.

He remembered he told the police he didn't see the bicycle, that he was aware there was a bike lane, that he looked before he turned. He remembered he signed a copy of his statement, then called Janet and asked for a ride.

"Did your truck break down?" she asked on the phone.

"No, I hit a guy on a bike. I just gave a statement to the police."

She arrived in ten minutes. Her face looked the way he felt. On the way home, she said, "My god, Ernie. What have you done?"

"It was an accident. I didn't see him. He must have come up beside me as I started my turn."

"Is he going to be okay?"

"I'm afraid not. He died on the way to the hospital."

"Oh, no. Dear God. This will ruin our lives."

"*Our* lives? The guy's dead, for Christ's sake."

"There's nothing you can do to change what happened to him. We have ourselves to worry about. Did you hit him while you were texting me?"

"No. Absolutely not."

She shook her head. "I knew this would happen someday. I *knew* it. You don't pay enough attention to your driving."

"Lay off. I feel bad enough."

"What will happen now?"

"I don't know. I may be charged, according to the police. Can we not talk about it until we get home?"

"Okay, but the first thing you do when we get home is call a lawyer."

"No lawyer," Ernie answered, adamant.

"What are you talking about?"

"We don't have the money."

"Your dad can help us."

"Are you kidding? He'd rather see me in jail. He won't give me a cent. Besides, I'd rather die than ask him. If I have to appear in court, I'll just explain what happened; I don't need a lawyer. Don't lecture me about this, Janet, I feel terrible about what happened, but look, how many times in my life have I heard, 'Ernie Farrell, you haven't lived up to your potential,' from my father, especially. Well, here's my chance to prove him wrong. I'll win the case on my own, no lawyer."

"You realize you might go to prison?"

"Nonsense. It was an accident. I won't go to prison."

Ernie wasn't as confident as he pretended to be. But what he told Janet was otherwise the truth. He felt sick to his stomach about the accident, but he could use it as a wake-up call to break out of his longstanding rut, a rut he had fallen into because of fear. He hadn't chosen a secondary life out of confidence or desire, he had chosen it out of fear that he couldn't live up to expectations.

He blamed his father – an outwardly avuncular man with a competitive instinct like you wouldn't believe; a man beloved by all except the people he had savaged in his relentless rise to the tippy-top of the financial heap; a man who preached that there was no such thing as try try again, there was only winning or disgrace. Ernie knew what his father would think when he heard about the accident: that Ernie had sullied the family name once again. Which was a joke considering that he, Ernie's dad, had spent twenty months in prison for insider trading a decade ago. True, his dad had rehabilitated his name by devoting himself to philanthropy after his release, but give me a break, Ernie thought.

*

Two miles away, newly retired judge Jim Randall formerly of the Massachusetts Superior Court sat in his darkened living room. He kept the front shades drawn at most hours, not because he was a recluse but because he lived on a busy street and the traffic going by his window was a distraction. Not a recluse? – his mind was the self-correcting kind, and after a brief but vigorous internal debate, he acknowledged he was part-recluse, concluding with the consoling thought that being part-recluse was no sin, especially in retirement. His natural tendency to withdraw had worsened since his dear wife, Joyce, passed away thirteen years ago. Her openness to others, her basic goodness, had worn off on him and made him a nicer man than he was. By nature, he was a bit of a grouch. Okay, he corrected himself, leave out the modifier: I am a grouch.

The phone rang. He much preferred landlines to cell phones: more reliable, harder to misplace. He rose from his easy chair and hobbled to the end table by the sofa. He hobbled not because of his size but because his legs stiffened when he sat for any length of time. He stood six two and weighed one ninety-five, only five pounds heavier than his fighting weight on the bench. He had not let himself go. His size, big head, and prominent features signaled gravitas, not sloth.

"Jim, it's Ted," he heard on the phone. "I need your advice." Ted Conover, Assistant District Attorney for Middlesex County. DA's came and went, Ted stayed and thrived. He essentially ran the office. He was an experienced trial lawyer and during the years when Jim was a judge, Ted had prosecuted many cases in Jim's court. A sixty-ish, laconic, straight arrow, Ted Conover always represented the Commonwealth with skill and honor, even when it meant clashing with Jim. Jim considered him a friend. During the year that Jim had been off the bench Ted occasionally sought his advice, as he did now. "I have a kid, Ernie Farrell...well, he's not a kid, he's thirty-one. Killed a BU student who was riding a bike. Chip on his shoulder, but I think he's terrified. Father wealthy but did time for insider trading. Here's the dilemma: a lot of Beacon Hill pols took campaign donations from the father and they still resent the way his conviction tainted them. They want to punish the father any way they can, and they see the son's trial as their chance. On top of that, the dead student's father is an up-by-the-boot-straps kind of guy from Somerville who became successful by building a chain of hardware stores that cater to the local community. He has plenty of friends on Beacon Hill. I'm under a lot of pressure to throw the book at young Ernie Farrell. That's okay with me as long as Farrell will cooperate with the public defender assigned to him, but I'm picking up signals that he won't. Maybe I'm a sap but I don't like shooting ducks in a barrel. Here's my question, Jim. You were legendary when you were on the bench for dissuading defendants from representing themselves. Refresh my memory, what was your secret? How did you get defendants to cooperate with the counsel assigned to them?"

"No secret. Carrot and stick. Make them believe you're sincerely interested in their well-being, then hit them with the dire consequences that will follow if they don't take your advice. Which judge has been assigned to the case?"

"Pat Knowles."

"She's good. I enjoyed serving with her. Have a bench conference with her and the public defender. Pat's a tough judge but she's fair, and she'll appreciate your concern."

"Thanks, Jim. You got good marks for saving fools from themselves. That's where your undeserved reputation for having a big heart got started."

"You're not to tell a soul what I'm really like," Jim said.

"Have I yet? In all the years we've known each other?"

"Ernie Farrell sounds like someone who is too proud to accept help, but you think the kid is guilty otherwise you wouldn't be proceeding."

"Guilty, yes, but not malicious. He seems scared and confused, and I don't want to put him away without a fair trial."

"Work with Pat Knowles. Between the two of you and the lawyer assigned to the case, you may be able to get through to the kid." Jim paused. "You knew all of this already, didn't you? You called because you miss my sweet disposition on the bench."

"I called mainly because I like talking to you, you old grouch."

"Who are you calling old? I have more hair than you."

"Hair is all you've got left. Take care, Jim."

He hung up, but didn't return to his chair. Instead, he went to the kitchen and poured himself a glass of wine – red, always red, preferably French and preferably from the Languedoc. He didn't consider white wine to be wine. His back window looked out at a jumble of multi-family houses beyond a parking lot shared by three houses. Joyce had been the one who wanted to move to the city. They had met in the Montpelier, Vermont District Attorney's office where they both were assistant DA's. Jim had been fresh out of law school, Joyce had a year of experience. They married three years later; two years after that Joyce brought to his attention an opening in a Boston law firm and Jim grabbed it. He wanted to try private practice while he was young, and she wanted to live in the city. A win-win.

He didn't know why Ted's phone call stuck in his mind. Maybe because he was bored. There, he had admitted it to himself. How pathetic, bored after only a year and a half of retirement. What had he been thinking when he left the bench at sixty-five, that he wouldn't miss it? That injustices would no longer infuriate him? I wanted to spend more time with my memories of Joyce, he reasoned with his cranky alter ego. But that was a load of crap. True, he was on the verge of forgetting her: not the big things, he'd never forget those – the little things, her quirks. The awkward way she cut her meat, like an apprentice carpenter. The certainty she was right coupled with crippling self-doubt. After trying unsuccessfully for years to have a child, they bought a second home overlooking the Connecticut River Valley north of Brattleboro, Vermont. Since Joyce's death, Jim made a point of going there as often as he could. Being there reminded him of her.

Maybe he should move to Vermont permanently. Now there's a thought; he was doing no good here.

Staring out the window, he surmised Ernie Farrell's motivation: rebellion, obstinacy, self-hatred. That was nuts, of course. Jim hadn't set eyes on the young man let alone learned much about him. How could he fathom his motivation? You've gone soft in the head in retirement, Randall, he told himself.

An idea hatched. Having nothing better to do tomorrow, why don't I go to the arraignment and check out the young man? Compare the actual Ernie Farrell to the Ernie Farrell of my fervid imagination.

It wasn't unheard of for Jim to appear at the courthouse. He stopped by from time to time, but his visits were infrequent enough that the clerks and lawyers did a minor-league double take whenever they saw him. "Mornin', Judge." "How you doing, Judge?" "Looking good, Judge."

To which Jim would smile benignly and mutter under his breath, 'bullshit.'

The arraignment was held in the courtroom where Jim had presided for many years. The spectator benches looked like church pews. He took a seat and checked out the other people in the courtroom. Ted Conover sat in the front row, leafing through documents. Across the aisle were a public defender and a slight young man with unruly hair and frightened eyes. The young man was trying without complete success to appear contemptuous of the proceedings. Cynical beyond his years.

The clerk called the name Ernest Farrell, and the young man and the lawyer assigned to his case stood.

"Are you representing Mr. Farrell?" Patricia Knowles, the presiding judge, was almost six feet tall, with the stern yet forgiving face of a Sunday school teacher who loves her students as long as they read their Bible lessons. She and Jim had served together for many years on the Superior Court. Defendants got a fair trial in her courtroom.

The public defender answered, "Your Honor, Mr. Farrell wants to represent himself. He refuses to cooperate with me."

"Is this true, Mr. Farrell?"

"Yes, Your Honor."

"You know that in so doing you are hurting yourself?"

"So I've been told."

"I've seen a lot of defendants represent themselves, and the number who have done a good job is zero."

"Then I can set a record, Your Honor."

Ted Conover spoke up. "Your Honor, may we approach the bench?"

Judge Knowles gestured the attorneys forward. She leaned down and listened intently to their whispers. After moment, she nodded. Ernie Farrell was still on his feet. The judge addressed him. "Mr. Farrell, you have the right to represent yourself, but I urge you once again to reconsider. The charge against you is vehicular homicide, a very serious charge. It could result in a prison sentence of up to fifteen years. We will proceed, but if before the trial you come to your senses and accept representation, you will be doing yourself a big favor. How do you plead, guilty or not guilty?"

"Not guilty."

A trial date and bail were set, and Ernie Farrell was free to leave. As he left the courtroom, Jim got a good look at him. His head was tucked between his shoulders as if he expected a blow from behind at any minute. There is hurt in his eyes, Jim thought. The hardened expression is a pose, a learned response to something he fears or hates.

Jim Randall was the most deliberate of men except when he wasn't, and he never knew when his latent impulsiveness (which sometimes approached impishness) would surface. Now he followed Ernie Farrell out of the courtroom and found him standing in the hallway arguing with a young woman. As Jim approached, Farrell stopped arguing with the woman and glared. "Who are you?"

"A retired judge, Jim Randall."

Farrell inspected Jim. "Don't I know you?"

"I don't think so," Jim replied.

Farrell snapped his fingers. "Now I remember. You were the judge in my case."

"I still don't remember."

"Well, I do. When I was nineteen. I knew you looked familiar. You were fair. I shoplifted two Radiohead CDs from Newbury Comics. You told me to do community service and stay out of trouble."

"Have you? Stayed out of trouble?"

"Yes, sir." He introduced the young woman he had been arguing with. "This is my wife, Janet."

Janet's scowl refused to budge. She shook Jim's hand. "He insists on representing himself. It makes me so mad. Can you talk sense into him?"

"I'll try. Mr. Farrell, you are doing yourself harm. I respect your reasons, but I suggest you reconsider."

"No one believes in me."

"Be that as it may, this isn't the time to prove them wrong."

"I disagree. This is the perfect time. I'll have Dad's full attention for the first time in my life." He seemed to reconsider. "I'll tell you what, Judge. If you agree to represent me, I'll drop my objections to a lawyer."

"That's not realistic. I'm retired from the bench and I have no experience as a defense attorney."

"But you could represent me if you wanted."

"Technically there's nothing stopping me. It's at the discretion of the presiding judge."

"Then would you?"

"I'm sure the lawyer assigned to you will do a good job, if you'll let him."

"You treated me like a human being. I trust you." He scribbled his phone number on a piece of paper. "Here. If you change your mind."

"I'm sorry. I urge you to reconsider your decision. Good luck."

Jim saw something of his younger self in Farrell. Jim had been a slacker in high school. He thought he was smarter than the kids who studied, that the kids who studied were saps. Then he almost flunked out of college. That turned him around. He studied his ass off and was admitted to Harvard Law School, where he excelled. He sensed the same mix of hubris and insecurity in Farrell. Guys like Farrell can go either way, work hard and do well, or crawl into a shell and blame the world.

"I want to help the kid," Jim thought to himself.

"Don't you dare," his cranky alter-ego said.

Jim's townhouse was halfway between Inman Square and Harvard Square in Cambridge. Since his retirement he spent most evenings in his third-floor study catching up on his reading: mostly history and current events. He didn't read one book at a time, he read several, darting from book to book like a broken-field runner. He absorbed information best that way. On the bench, he had to focus on the matter at hand. He had the discipline to do so, but the effort mentally wore him down, in contrast to the exuberance he felt when his mind was free to wander.

What made Ernie Farrell tick? This was the kind of thing he would endlessly discuss with Joyce when she was alive. Joyce had none of his scholarly bent but oodles of human savvy. He mentally tried an idea on her now (his habit when he was alone): Ernie Farrell thinks he's fated to lose in life and the trial gives him to chance to sneer at his father while losing. You mean he loves his father too much to want to humiliate him but is tired of not standing up for himself (she clarified). Exactly. She was so smart.

A second later, he realized he was alone in a room with his reading lamp glaring off the page and the pain of missing Joyce as poignant as ever. He was beginning to think something was wrong with him. When Joyce had died, friends and acquaintances assured him that while the pain would never vanish, eventually it would ebb, its edges become less sharp, but it hadn't, not really, and he wondered if he was carrying loyalty too far. Loyalty was a good thing, he believed, but hiding behind a deceased wife's memory for thirteen years could be a form of denial.

He sat still long enough for his mind to empty of conscious thought. Gradually a critical mass of an idea took shape and he was propelled out of his chair to the phone by a moral imperative that overpowered resistence.

"Ernie Farrell?" he said when a young man answered the phone.

"Yes? Who is this?"

"Judge Randall. I've changed my mind. I'll represent you."

2

Being a horrible cook, Jim ate out a lot. His favorite restaurant was Duck, Duck, Goose, a small bistro around the corner from his townhouse. Thirty-six covers at nine tables, eight at a horseshoe bar. The owner was a cherubic-faced young man from Brooklyn named Bruce. Bruce wore a goatee, which Jim deemed a mistake: the face a boy's, the goatee a man's. In addition to its convenient location, Jim kept returning to Duck, Duck, Goose because Bruce and the bartender/counterman Chris accommodated Jim's timid taste buds, always having at least one plain dish on the menu (or on special order for Judge Randall): chicken, a simply prepared fish.

Jim wanted to meet with Farrell to prepare for the trial, but before he did, he needed to brush up on the law of vehicular homicide. He found the counter at Duck, Duck, Goose a congenial place to do so. The staff had standing orders to protect his privacy if he wanted to read. Tucked into the corner of the horseshoe counter with his iPad and his glass of Languedoc, Jim boned up on the dry details of death by automobile.

The crux of the matter was negligence. Gross negligence leading to the death of another was a felony, simple negligence a misdemeanor. Ernie had been charged with gross negligence.

A lot depended on the judge, as it always did. The law does a pretty good job of extracting personality from its deliberations, but no human endeavor is devoid of personality. Here Jim had an advantage. When Pat Knowles lost her spouse soon after Jim lost his, they fell into a routine of commiserating over lunch in the courthouse cafeteria. It never amounted to anything other than colleagues supporting each other in their grief but while it lasted, they were an 'item' in courthouse gossip. They lost touch after Jim retired but their mutual sympathy remained.

"Another?" The voice was that of the Chris, the bartender.

Jim looked at his wine glass. He hadn't realized it was empty. "Sure. Thanks."

Chris was even younger than Bruce. He was very serious about terroir. Get him started on the subject and he could go on for hours.

"Food will be here soon, Judge."

"About time." Jim noticed that half the stools at the counter had filled up while he was preoccupied. "I was beginning to think of suing Duck, Duck, Goose."

"For what?" Chris asked in all seriousness.

"Contempt of court."

"I thought you were retired."

"I was making a joke, Chris."

Chris began to wipe a glass. "I knew that."

A young woman deposited Jim's plate in front of him with a breezy, "Enjoy!"

*

At his Somerville apartment, Ernie Farrell didn't know what to make of Judge Randall's change of mind.

"I thought you'd be happy," Janet, his wife, said at the kitchen table. She was a year younger than Ernie but looked older.

"I am."

"You don't look it. You look rattled."

"What if I lose?"

"You didn't consider that before?"

"Sure, I did, but the whole thing seemed like a joke until now."

Their apartment was in a dense section of Somerville, one town over from Cambridge. Somerville historically was a blue-collar family town, but artists and techies had moved in, and now the multi-family houses lining the streets had more easels than strollers.

"Motor vehicle homicide by negligent operation. Homicide. Can you believe it? I'm not guilty. You know how crazy bike riders are. They think they're cowboys on the open range. I didn't see him."

"Did you look?"

"I *told* you. Yes, I looked."

"Were you texting?"

"No, I ended my text to you before I turned."

"Did you have your turn signal on?"

"I don't remember. Goddamn it. Why the third degree?"

Ernie was used to being falsely accused. Growing up, he had served as a magnet for his father's frequent fury and his mother's constant regrets. By adulthood, it became a chicken-and-egg question: was he defensive because accusations unerringly sought him out, or did accusations seek him because he was defensive? He had been an awkward child and an angry teen but had settled down at community college and done well enough to finish his BA at Northeastern. He was tired of being a punching bag.

He was meeting with Judge Randall in the morning. He never dreamed that the Judge would agree to represent him. Now that he had, Ernie had to take the chip off his shoulder and cooperate.

They met at The Long Gone, a coffee shop in Inman Square. The Long Gone had once been a jazz club and still attracted an eclectic, arty crowd. The decor was next to nothing, the ambience unappealing, which was precisely what was cool about it. In a coffee shop like The Long Gone, no one notices an odd couple like a fidgety young man and a scowling older man with a craggy face.

Jim got there first and sat down at a rear table with his dark roast. For a man who lived by routine, who craved regularity, Jim switched coffees remarkably often. He scanned *The New York Times* while he waited, the only patron reading a print newspaper, although The Long Gone had a supply of them on the front windowsill. He was engrossed in an article on New York City corruption when he glimpsed the torso of a man standing by the table and realized young Ernie Farrell had snuck up on him.

"Morning." Jim gestured at the empty chair.

Ernie sat. "Sorry I'm late."

"I was early. I live nearby."

Jim took a second to size up Ernie. He looked different than in court. More frightened, less defiant. Jim thought he knew what the kid lacked. First he's got to take the chip off his shoulder.

Ernie pulled his chair closer. "May I ask you something?"

"Sure."

"Why did you change your mind and take my case?"

Tell the truth? What was the truth? That I'm bored in retirement, and why not see if I've still got it? To help a kid who reminds me of my younger self? Maybe not the truth, the whole truth and nothing but the truth, but close enough for a coffee shop that once reverberated with the sounds of jazz.

Jim answered simply, "Something about your case intrigued me."

"It wasn't because of my father?"

"No."

"Do you know who he is?"

"Yes. A man of wealth and political influence who did time for insider trading."

"He didn't put you up to this?"

"Good god, no. I've never met or talked to him."

"He's used to getting his way."

"Mr. Farrell, I do not know your father. I have never communicated with your father. Even if I had, he couldn't influence me. I make up my own mind."

"Mr. Farrell is my dad's name. Call me Ernie."

"Ernie it is. And when we meet in The Long Gone, you can call me Jim. Not in court, though. In court, I'm Judge Randall."

"Yes, sir."

"Shall we start?"

For the next hour, Jim questioned Ernie about the accident – what Ernie saw, what he did, what he heard. Jim avoided direct questions about fault. He wanted to put Ernie at ease, wanted to establish baseline facts.

To question a client felt foreign to Jim. For over twenty years, it had been other people's job to ask the questions, his to sit in judgement. It was a difficult transition to make, but not impossible. He struggled not to pass judgement on what he was hearing.

"So what do you think?" Ernie asked at the end of the hour.

"What troubles me most is your texting."

"But I wasn't texting when we collided."

"There's only your word for that. If the DA can connect your texting to the accident, you'll be found guilty."

Ernie went into the emotional equivalent of a defensive crouch. Jim noticed. "Don't bristle. I believe you, but it's the DA who matters. One final question, were you aware there was a bicycle on your right?"

"I saw him a couple of blocks back. He whizzed by me at a red light, then he dropped back. Goddamn bikes think they own the fucking road."

"And we shall practice not saying fucking in court, agreed? So you didn't see him as you turned?"

"No. I looked but I didn't see him. I told you."

"Some questions need to be repeated. I think we're done for today. When you get home, look in the mirror and remove the chip from your shoulder. Use a chisel if you have to. Here's my card. Call me if you think of anything you forgot to tell me."

Ernie looked at the card. "What do you think my chances are?"

"Too early to tell. For one thing, I have to decide whether we should waive your right to a jury trial. You may be better off having Judge Knowles decide the case. I served on the bench with her. She's excellent at deciding on fact, not emotion."

"But do I have a chance?"

"Yes, or I wouldn't have taken the case."

Ernie nodded. "I'm married, I'm employed, I have a future. I'm not a danger to anybody. Going to prison wouldn't serve any purpose."

"Don't think about prison. Concentrate instead on remembering anything that might help me in court. No detail is too small."

Ernie stopped halfway to his feet. "You haven't mentioned money. I can't afford much, and I won't ask my father for help."

"We'll talk about money later. I'm not doing this for money."

"Really?"

"Really. We'll meet again here in a couple of days. I need to do some digging."

Jim often walked head down, as if fascinated by his feet. He did so on the way home from The Long Gone, but feet were the last thing on his mind. He was replaying all the signals he received from Ernie Farrell. He read Ernie to be a rattled young man, not the hardened kind of defendant he had often seen in court. True, Ernie had an attitude, but his underlying personality was earnest and genuine, if Jim read him correctly.

Jim passed Cambridge Hospital. He had just left a young man with his life before him and was passing the place where his wife had died. He had thought of death more often since he retired. Maybe he had taken Ernie's case to keep his mind on life.

3

Jim spent the weekend at his house in Vermont, reading the law of vehicular homicide. Like many aspects of the law, much depended on statutes and cases that bore no inherent connection to vehicles or homicide – the terms "reckless" and "negligent", for example. Both terms were the focus of voluminous case law covering a vast array of situations. Yes, a lot of law was codified in statutes but once a law was passed much depended on subsequent court cases to refine, define, and clarify it.

Reading the vehicular homicide law as a trial lawyer instead of as a judge was a culture shock for Jim. For part of the weekend, he feared he had made a grave mistake taking Ernie Farrell's case, feared he couldn't do a good job for the young man. He consoled himself by remembering that Ernie had planned to represent himself. Even a flawed performance by Jim would be better than Ernie representing himself.

He liked to take long walks when he was in Vermont. The little house which he and Joyce had bought thirty years ago sat just below the crest of a high ridge with a view to the east. A silver sliver of river could be glimpsed in the distance when lighting conditions were right. The time when that occurred fascinated him. It wasn't when you'd think – when the sun was at its brightest or directly overhead. It seemed to have to do with angles: the angle the light glanced off the water. He was pretty sure he could

Google a quick explanation of the behavior of light, but that would remove the quiet pleasure of pondering the how and whys.

When he got back to the house from Saturday's walk, he saw Jake and Casey Allen's pickup in the driveway. Jake and Casey were the youngish couple who looked after the house when Jim was in Cambridge. Jake was a jack-of-all-trades and Casey had a degree in early childhood education but found she preferred moving from job to job, house to house, helping Jake with a variety of tasks, to doing one thing in one place. Jim wasn't sure of their ages but guessed they were in their mid to late thirties. Both were tall and trim, with muscles that Jim had never dreamed of having. As far as Jim could tell, between them they could do everything.

Jake got out of the pickup when he saw Jim coming. "Hey, Judge. Didn't expect you this weekend."

"Spur of the moment thing," Jim exclaimed. "What brings you here on a Saturday?"

"Case and I are on our way to a tag sale and decided to check on the gas odor I emailed you about. Have you noticed anything?"

"Nope. But then again, my nostrils are shot."

"Mind if I go in and check?"

"Be my guest."

While Jake was inside the house, Jim talked to Casey. Casey had short hair and a quick smile. He liked her eyes – a pale blue with hints of some other color, green or gray? His color sense was as bad as his sense of smell.

"How are things going?" he asked.

"Fine, Judge. Good to see you. Up for the weekend?"

"Yep. Researching a case for a client."

"I thought you were retired."

"I am. I volunteered to represent a young man in court."

Jake emerged from the house and approached the pickup. "No odor. I had the gas company check it out while you were gone, but gas is one of those things that can sneak up on you. Ready to move on?" Jake asked Casey.

"Let's be on our way."

Jake got in the driver's side. "See you, Judge."

"Take care, you two." Jim waved and went inside the house.

The house was small – cozy, Joyce called it. They had talked about adding a room, but having no children and rarely inviting guests, they didn't need additional space.

Their time together was mostly spent in solitary pursuits – Jim, reading briefs or history; Joyce, straightening knickknacks, knitting – physical proximity and an occasional comment were all he needed to feel at ease. Jim had work friends like Pat Knowles, but by personal inclination and the need to keep a distance between himself and anyone who might appear before him in court, he had few outside friends and liked it that way. Since Joyce's death, he was delighted they had kept the Vermont house small and personal. He hadn't done a thing to it since she died.

Nights alone were tough at first. He had gotten used to sleeping alone but missed the way Joyce breathed when asleep. There was a purposefulness to it, a 'let's get this job done and get on with it' impatience to it. She seemed calmer awake than asleep, which never ceased to amaze him.

*

Back in Cambridge on Monday morning, he went as usual to The Long Gone. The coffee shop was half full. The before-work crowd had moved out and the lunch crowd hadn't arrived. Ernie Farrell sat across from Jim looking pensive.

"What's wrong?" Jim asked.

"Janet. She's being a serious asshole. Says I'll make a bad impression in court and people won't believe me. Will they?"

"There's no way of knowing how a person will do on the witness stand. I've seen confident people break down, meek people do well. Besides, I may not put you on the witness stand."

Ernie seemed disturbed to hear that. "You won't?"

"I may not," Jim said. "The decision whether or not to put a defendant on the witness stand is a tactical one. Depends how the trial has gone up to that point. I've been reviewing your case, here's what I've learned so far. The police lab found no evidence of intoxication, which is very good. If you had been intoxicated, you could spend up to fifteen years in prison. If found guilty of negligent homicide without intoxication, the sentence is usually much less. The wild card is the texting. There's a law on the books making texting while driving illegal per se, but the law is brand new and there's no telling how it will be applied. It will take time for a case law to emerge."

"Janet blames me for getting in this mess."

"She needs to lighten up. The trial will not always go smoothly. Ted Conover is a fair-minded individual, but in court, he is determined."

*

A week later, Ted Conover called Jim to tell him he was forwarding an inventory of the evidence in the Farrell case. Some DAs get so used to peering under rocks and seeing vermin scurry away that they think everyone is hiding something. Not Ted; Ted sized up people fairly, assuming neither the best nor the worst, letting their actions speak for themselves, only occasionally letting his temper show. Not that he didn't like to win, In court he was a dogged opponent, but he wasn't a zealot like some prosecutors.

The evidence when it arrived revealed that Ernie had texted Janet at 8:43 p.m. the evening of the accident. The first call to 911 occurred at 8:53 p.m. Eyewitness accounts of the time of the accident varied from 8:30 to 9. A shopkeeper across the road who heard the crash checked his watch, it read 8:48. The police report estimated the time of the accident as 8:45.

If texting were found to be a contributing cause of the accident, Pat Knowles might impose a harsh sentence under the new law. Working in Ernie's favor was the lack of precision in determining the time of the accident. If the trial seemed to be going against Ernie, Jim might suggest pleading guilty to a lesser charge which did not include a prison sentence.

He broached the idea to Ernie at their next Long Gone meeting.

"No way," was Ernie's instant answer.

Jim was surprised by his vehemence. "I'm not saying we plea-bargain now. I'm saying we keep the idea in our back pocket."

"I won't plead guilty when I'm not."

"Ernie, are you going to be this stubborn the whole trial? Just keep the possibility of an eventual plea bargain in mind."

"If I plead guilty, it will prove that every bad thought my father's had about me has been right. When he was on trial for insider trading, he refused to plea-bargain, claiming he was scapegoated for the crimes of Wall Street. For me to plead guilty to a crime would disgrace the family, that's how he would see it."

The chatter in the Long Gone this morning was louder than usual. Jim said, "Let me get this straight. You're willing to risk jail time because you're afraid of your dad?"

"Not afraid. Doing what I think is right. My answer to Dad is fuck you, Dad."

Jim was slightly annoyed. "He's not here, he can't hear you."

Ernie raised his voice. "Fuck you, Dad!"

Nearby patrons glanced up from their phones and laptops, saw a young man cursing an older man they presumed to be his father, and returned to their screens with no change of expression.

4

Jim had one living relative, his sister Natalie. She was six years younger than he and lived on the Oregon coast. Since their mother had died twenty years ago, neither Natalie nor Jim made the transcontinental crossing more than every couple of years. But they kept in touch, not often but enough. When they did, it meant a lot to Jim. Natalie was fond of everyone she met; a woman of open arms and steady gaze. She was married to a peach of a man, Stuart.

Jim called her now, catching her just after dinner. "We just finished. Stu's cleaning up," she explained when Jim asked if he was interrupting.

"I can hear him."

Stu was whistling as he washed.

"What's up?" Natalie asked.

"Am I crazy? I agreed to defend a young man accused of vehicular homicide."

"You agreed to be his lawyer?"

"Pro bono."

"You *are* crazy, but this sounds like you: stubborn and wedded to routine one day, then impulsive and foolhardy as a child the next. It's one thing I love about you."

"Tell me the others."

Natalie had two laughs: a burst of hilarity when least expected and a chortle deep in her throat. Now she chortled. "Your need for compliments." She paused to tell Stu to put his dirty dish in the dishwasher. "Not in the cabinet, dear." Then on the phone, she asked Jim, "Do you want me to psychoanalyze you?"

"I'll save you the trouble. My client reminds me of myself when I was young, therefore by helping him I am helping a younger version of myself."

"Very good. And you want me to confirm you are doing the right thing."

"Am I?"

"You haven't tried a case in, what, thirty years? And you were a prosecutor, not a defense attorney. Can you do a good job?"

"That is the question."

"Typical Jim. High stakes are usually involved when you get impulsive. The higher the stakes, the more of a risk taker you become. Hold on, I'm going to move into the other room."

A moment later, she came back on the line. "I didn't want Stu to hear this. He doesn't know yet, but I'm thinking of taking early retirement to care for him." Natalie was a physical therapist and loved her work. Giving it up could only mean one thing.

"His Alzheimer's getting worse?"

"Yes. He has to be closely watched. I hate to quit my job, but if I have to, I will."

"I'm sorry, very sorry. For both of you."

"Don't be, I'm lucky. You don't have anybody who needs you. I'd hate to be in your shoes."

*

"Good morning, Your Honor." Jim and Ted Conover greeted Patricia Knowles in her courthouse chambers. Judge Knowles on the bench was a formidable figure but in her chambers she was approachable, if business-like. She had dark brown hair which she apparently paid no attention to besides cutting once in a while.

"Good morning, counselors. Let's get one question out of the way. In considering whether to allow Jim to appear before me for the defense, I weighed the possibility that I would be biased in favor of a former colleague. I decided that I can judge the case fairly, but I'll listen to arguments to the contrary."

"One more thing," Jim interjected. "Early in my judicial career, I heard a case of shoplifting in which a very young Mr. Farrell was the defendant. I had forgotten it until Mr. Farrell reminded me."

"Mr Conover? Does that disturb you?"

"No, Your Honor. I have confidence in your ability to judge this case on its merits regardless of who represents the defendant."

Pat Knowles nodded. "Given the time that has passed, and given that in this case Jim will be representing the defendant instead of judging him, and given that the defendant refuses to let anyone but Jim defend him and a client representing himself is the worst possible scenario, under the circumstances Jim may proceed. When will the two of you be ready?"

"We're ready now, Your Honor," Conover said.

"Jim?"

"I request another month, Your Honor."

"Done. The clerk of the court will set a date. Have you decided whether you'll seek a jury?" she asked Jim.

"No, we haven't decided yet."

"Very well. Anything else, gentlemen?"

Ted glanced at Jim. "You doing okay?"

"How do you mean?"

"I don't know. We've known each other a long time. Just asking."

"I'm doing fine."

Pat Knowles said, "I think Ted is saying he's glad you took the case, and I am too."

Ted nodded.

"Thanks. I'm glad I took the case, too. It'll feel good to be back in court. The question is, will Ernie Farrell be glad after the case is over?"

Pat stood to put on her robe. Jim smiled tightly. "It makes we weepy to see you don your robe."

"Maybe you retired too soon."

"Could be."

He walked home through East Cambridge. A long walk but doable. He loved the mom-and-pop stores along the street – Rosie's House of Beauty; Carol's Hair and Nails; a barber shop that also made money transfers; a live poultry store with hyperactive chickens in the window. Store signs in Spanish, Portugese, and Korean. There was more life in any block of Cambridge Street than in all of fabled Brattle Street on the other side of Harvard Square.

Had he retired too soon? Not that the question hadn't occurred to him, but to hear Pat Knowles say it hit home. A thought: win Ernie Farrell's case and build a tidy second career as a trial lawyer. He could pick and choose his cases, take only those that interested him, and spend the rest of the time in Vermont. Alone. His love of Joyce had been enough for a lifetime, but he missed the company of women.

Jim fixed himself dinner that night. Prepared meat loaf from the corner market warmed in the microwave for thirty seconds, and frozen peas. He liked peas. Why weren't they served in restaurants more often?

When he ate at home he watched the PBS Newshour, the only news show on TV worth watching. God forbid he watched FOX or even MSNBC. Jim leaned toward MSNBC's views but hated to be hectored, especially at dinner. And two glasses of red wine from the Languedoc, preferably Minervois or Corbières.

Strategy was on his mind. Whether to focus on ruling out texting as the accident's cause or focus on negligence more broadly. It didn't have to be one or the other, but which to highlight? Which to start with? A lot would depend on the prosecution's case. If he knew Ted Conover as well as he thought he did, Ted would start slowly then build in tempo and intensity. It was an effective way to gain a jury's confidence, which led directly to the most important decision: jury trial or trial by judge? He found himself leaning towards the latter. A jury could be swayed by Ernie's negative attitude while Pat Knowles was more likely to decide based solely on the facts and the law.

One trick he had learned years ago when faced with a close call was to make a tentative decision and live with it overnight. His tentative decision? To waive a jury.

The decision still felt right the next morning when he met with Ernie. The coffee of the day at The Long Gone was caramel pecan mocha. Ernie's reaction to waiving a jury was a shrug.

"No reaction?" Jim asked.

Ernie, petulant. "You're the lawyer."

"But you're the one on trial."

"I'm okay with it, if that's what you want to hear."

"Ernie, you have to stop shrugging like a high schooler caught smoking a joint in the john whenever we discuss the trial. This is serious stuff."

Ernie stretched his neck, which jutted his chin. "I'm tired of being on the defensive."

"That's just the point. You'll be on the defensive until the verdict is rendered. That's what comes with being a defendant."

Ernie shrugged.

"There you go again. Cut it out."

"Okay."

"I mean it. Even if you feel contemptuous about being put on trial, keep in mind that the young man on the bike is dead. If you sound or look dismissive in court, Ted Conover will eviscerate you."

"You've made your point."

"Be magnanimous, sound like you care."

"I do."

"Then show it."

"Okay."

"So you're fine with waiving a jury?"

Dismissively, "You're the boss."

Jim exploded. "Stop with the goddamn tone!"

"Sorry. Habit."

"A bad one. Break it."

In measured tones, Ernie said, "It's just that I'm scared."

"That's better."

"I'm fine with waiving a jury."

"Good. I'll tell Judge Knowles."

5

Press interest in the case heated up as the trial approached – 'Son of Convicted Investment Banker Stands Trial In Death Of College Student' – i.e., the apple doesn't fall far from the tree. That the deceased, Vincent Degregorio, Jr., had been a promising student and well liked ("greatest guy in the world, he'd do anything for you") added to the drama. On the trial's opening day, Jim spotted a dozen journalists in the courtroom. Ernie Farrell's wife Janet sat in the first row, directly behind Ernie and Jim at the defense table. No other relatives of Ernie's attended. Friends and family of the deceased bicyclist filled five rows behind Ted Conover at the prosecutor's table.

As the courtroom waited for Judge Knowles to enter, Jim glanced at Ernie, who looked as if a priest had given him last rites and a black hood was about to be placed over his head. Jim whispered to him, "You okay?"

"All rise." The spectators rose as Judge Knowles swept through the rear door and ascended the bench. She surveyed the courtroom, then instructed, "Please sit. Clerk will read the indictment."

How many times had Jim mounted the bench like that, said those very words, adjusted his thinking from private citizen to judge? How many times had he wanted to announce before he began: 'I, a fallible man, am about to pronounce judgement on a fellow human being. Forgive me for I know not what I do.' He had a role to play, and he had learned over the years to play it well. The mistakes he made – too many to count – he regretted, deeply regretted in some cases, but overall he looked back on his career with muted satisfaction. He judged himself to have been a better than average judge, but by no means the best. What wouldn't he give to be on the bench today instead of sitting beside the defendant? How he envied Pat Knowles with her robe and gavel. She was speaking to him. Pay attention, Jim.

"The court has received a form from counsel for the defense saying the defendant wishes to waive a jury, and that the defendant has been informed by counsel of his right to a jury of his peers. Is that correct?"

Jim half-rose from the table. "Yes, Your Honor."

"Mr. Farrell, is it your wish to waive your right to a jury and have your case tried by me?"

"Yes."

"Please stand when you address the court. Thank you. Mr. Farrell do you understand by so doing that you are waiving your constitutional right to be tried by a jury of your peers?"

Ernie – on his feet – replied, "Yes, ma'am, Your Honor."

"Is your decision made under pressure from your counsel or the District Attorney's office, or any other person?"

"No, Your Honor."

"And do you make this decision free from the influence of alcohol or drugs?"

"Yes, Your Honor."

"Then we will proceed without a jury. Mr. Farrell, please sign the form your attorney has filled out and give it to the court clerk."

When Ernie had so done, Judge Knowles said, "Mr. Conover, you may proceed with your opening statement."

Ted Conover rose. He looked trim, ready. "May it please the court." He recited the dry facts of the case, then previewed his argument. "Your Honor, it is an unfortunate fact of modern life that traffic accidents happen and that people die in those accidents. Sometimes those accidents are the result of bad luck – dense fog, a blown tire, slick roads. Sometimes the accidents are caused by the deliberate actions of a driver. But other times the accidents are caused by carelessness, not on purpose or by chance. The case law on negligence is already voluminous, but technology has added a whole new chapter. Smart phones make drivers do dumb things, and the law is playing catch-up."

Ted Conover stepped out from behind the prosecutor's table. He moved with the right degree of sureness to convey confidence without arrogance. "Your Honor, the Massachusetts Legislature recently passed and the Governor signed into law, a statute that makes texting while driving illegal in and of itself, even if no other law has been breached. The case law governing vehicular homicide does not yet reflect this change, and it is up to the courts to flesh out the meaning and limits of the new statute by applying it to actual fact situations. The case before the court today breaks new ground. That is what makes it so important."

He returned to his place and rested his hands on the back of his chair. "The Commonwealth will argue that the facts of this case constitute negligence, but we will also contend that the addition of texting to the facts makes the negligence in this case especially egregious and warrants a penalty that will set an example for those who follow. I have nothing further at this point, Your Honor."

"Thank you. Mr. Randall?"

Jim stood. Good opening statement, he thought as he buttoned his coat; short and to the point.

"Good morning, Your Honor." Jim moved out from behind the defense table. "Your Honor, the defense will argue that the death in this case was a tragic accident, not the result of negligence or intent, but in no way do we minimize the grievous loss that the family and friends of the deceased have suffered. The defendant would give anything if he could undo the events that led to this tragedy." Jim stepped forward until he was clear of the table. His body felt ponderous. No bench to hide behind, no robe to wear, no gavel to wield.

"The crux of this case is lack of proof. The timeline is murky, physical evidence lacking, eyewitness testimony conflicting, and fault unclear. For negligence to be established, there must be more than supposition, there must be supporting evidence. No guesses, no approximations. Evidence. This standard is especially important where a felony is charged, the penalties are stiff, and the stigma is lasting. We will examine the facts in detail after the prosecution presents its case. For now, the defense is ready to proceed." Jim returned to his seat.

"Thank you, Judge Randall. You may call your first witness, Mr. Conover."

The first police officer to arrive at the scene took the stand. After raising his right hand, he painstakingly reported what he had observed: a crumbled bike, a distraught Ernie Farrell, horrified onlookers, EMT's arriving a moment later and extracting the victim from beneath Ernie's pickup. The direct questioning took an hour. When it ended, Jim rose to cross-examine. "Officer, can you please describe the defendant's manner when you arrived on the scene?"

"Distraught. Scared. Upset."

"Cocky?"

"No, sir. He seemed genuinely horrified by what had happened."

"Did you observe any signs of intoxication?"

"No, sir."

"Did you conduct a breathalyzer test?"

"Yes. It's routine in such cases."

"Did the breathalyzer test show signs of intoxication?"

"No, sir, it did not."

Jim plucked a document off the defense table. "Officer, did your accident report say who was to blame?"

"No, sir."

"Why not?"

"It was impossible from a quick visual inspection of the accident scene to ascertain."

"You did not state the probable cause of the accident?"

"No, sir. That was not my job. The forensics team handles that."

"Thank you. No further questions."

Methodically, patiently, Ted Conover called other police officers, EMT's, and a forensic expert to the witness stand and by the end of the day, the following facts had been entered in the record. Short skid marks from the bicycle were found in the bike lane, no skid marks from the pickup were found. There was no indication from the physical evidence that either the pickup or the bicycle was traveling outside their designated lanes. Excessive speed was not involved, nor was intoxication. The defendant had sent a text message to his wife at 8:43 p.m. The first call to 911 occurred at 8:53. The police estimate of the time of accident was 8:45.

Jim took himself to Duck, Duck, Goose for dinner that evening. He had plenty of work to do but needed a breather. He ate at the counter.

"Evenin', Judge," Chris said. "You look exhausted. Everything okay?"

"Long day, Chris."

Chris brought him a Cote du Rhone Villages on the house. Jim tipped his glass to Chris. He felt like an out-of-shape athlete. The day as a litigator had drained him far more than a day on the bench. He consoled himself by saying he had done okay for the first day. Of course, this was a day of laying the groundwork for what was to come, and what was to come wouldn't be so easy.

He skipped a second glass of wine and went home to prepare for the next day. The big question was how closely Ted Conover would be able to tie the texting to the collision. From the testimony so far, there was no conclusive proof of cause and effect, but Conover was a good lawyer and undoubtably would do his best to link the two.

The main decision Jim would later face was whether to put Ernie on the witness stand. When Ernie lowered his guard, he was an appealing young man but his guard was up so much of the time it had become ingrained. Would Ernie be able to drop his sneer for the duration of his testimony if Jim put him on the stand?

Jim stayed up until midnight, then slept soundly. In the morning he felt at peace with himself in an anxious sort of way.

"Why do I feel at peace?" he asked the Joyce in his head. One of the hardest parts of losing her had been the abrupt end to the running conversation that is a marriage. Eventually he decided to carry on the conversation whether or not she was there. As long as I know I'm doing it, I'm not dotty, he rationalized.

As was often the case, asking her a question provided the answer. Joyce: You feel at peace because you're back in court. Jim: But a young man's future is at stake. I have no right to feel at peace. Joyce: You always felt more at home in court than elsewhere, why should it be different now?

The air felt good when he got off the bus near the courthouse. Crisp and new. He walked briskly, feeling a surge of what he could only call youth. Why he felt revitalized he couldn't say; second day adrenalin? Fewer spectators today, which made the half empty courtroom look shabby. He placed his notes on the defense table and waited for Ernie to arrive.

Ernie did a moment later, leading Janet by a step. He did not look at her before he sat at the defense table, nor did she say anything to him before she sat in the spectator section.

"Everything okay?" Jim asked after Ernie didn't greet him.

"Wonderful."

"If you two are having a fight, keep it to yourselves. Judge Knowles notices."

Ernie almost spat. "A man can't argue with his wife?"

"Yes, he can. And a man can go to jail if he brings the argument to court with him."

Ernie turned and nodded to Janet. To Jim, he said, "Satisfied?"

Ted Conover was in his seat, as were the court clerk and bailiffs. Pat Knowles swept through the door by the bench, her robe a spinnaker, and the trial resumed.

The prosecution's first witness was a young woman who didn't look eager to testify. The first questions established her name as Irene Rossario, that she was a grad student at Suffolk University, and that she had been waiting for a bus across the street from the interstate entrance at the time of the accident.

"Ms. Rossario," Ted Conover began, "Did you observe anything out of the ordinary as you were waiting?"

"Yes, I did."

"Tell the court what you observed."

Irene Rossario had a tentative manner. "I saw a pickup truck hit a man on a bicycle."

"Did you observe who was driving the pickup truck?"

"Yes."

"Is that person in the courtroom?"

"Yes, he is."

"Will you please point him out?"

Ms. Rossario pointed at Ernie. "Him."

"You are pointing at the defendant?"

"Yes, sir."

"How can you be sure it was him?"

"He got out of his truck after the accident. I got a good look at him."

"Ms. Rossario, did you see the accident happen?"

"Yes, I did."

"Please describe what you observed."

"I saw the defendant looking down at his lap just before he began the turn. I saw the bicycle collide with the truck. It was awful." She tried to shake the memory out of her head.

"Take your time."

"I saw the defendant stop his truck and get out to see what had happened. He came around to the other side of the truck, and I couldn't see what he did, but after that he got back into his truck and appeared to call somebody on his phone."

"Thank you. Your witness," Conover said to Jim.

Jim stood and buttoned his coat. His tone was gentle. "I know this is hard for you, Ms. Rossario, but can you tell us what you were doing just before the accident?"

"I was waiting for the bus."

"And what were you doing while you were waiting for the bus?"

"I was talking to my friend, Jill."

"Was Jill with you?"

"No, sir. I was talking to her on my phone."

"While you were talking to a friend on the phone as you waited for a bus, I assume you were paying close attention to the traffic?"

"No, sir, not close attention."

"Would it be fair to say your mind was elsewhere?"

"Yes, sir, that's fair."

"Was there a normal amount of traffic that evening?"

"No, sir. There was heavier than usual traffic."

"And it's a busy street even on a normal evening, is that correct?"

"Yes, I would say so."

Jim paced a few steps forward and back. He rubbed his chin and said nothing, then stopped and looked at the witness. "Let me get this straight. You were chatting with your friend on the phone while you waited for a bus on a day when the traffic was heavier than usual, and you glanced up and just happened to notice one particular driver looking down at his lap before he made a turn?"

"Yes, sir."

Jim took the forensics report from the table. "Ms. Rossario, I'd like you to look at this sketch of the scene, which has been entered into evidence as part of the police report on the accident." Jim handed her the sketch. "Familiarize yourself with it, and I'll ask you a few questions."

Ms. Rosario studied the sketch. The courtroom was silent. Jim stood still until she looked up.

"Finished?"

"Yes, sir."

Jim stepped forward. "Now, can you point on the map to where you were standing?"

"Yes, sir. Here."

Jim looked where she was pointing. "You are pointing at a spot diagonally across the street from where the accident occurred. Is that correct?"

"Yes, sir."

"May I?" Jim took the sketched map from her and held it up for the judge to see. "Your Honor, the spot where Ms. Rosario was standing is at an obtuse angle to where the accident happened. To my untrained eye it looks to be approximately a 120 degree angle."

Judge Knowles leaned down to get a better look. When satisfied, she nodded, "Show the prosecution."

Jim took the map to the prosecution table. Ted Conover and his assistant studied it for a moment. After they had a look, Jim took the map to the defense table and turned again towards the witness.

"Ms. Rosario, I ask you again. Are you sure you could accurately see where the defendant was looking as he made his turn?"

She faltered. "I know what I remember."

Jim stepped back behind the table. "I'm not challenging what you remember, Ms. Rossario. You are here in good faith. What I am suggesting is that when a person is talking on the phone while waiting for a bus amidst a lot of traffic noise and confusion and watching diagonally across the street as a pickup truck made a turn, the person's memory of exactly what happened may be inaccurate."

Ted Conover stood. "Objection, Your Honor. Mr. Randall is making his closing argument."

"I am cross-examining the witness. Wider latitude is allowed during cross-examination, as Mr. Conover knows."

"Objection overruled. But be cautious, Mr. Randall. Remember which side of the bench you're on."

"Seeing you on the bench instead of me, Your Honor, how could I forget?"

Judge Knowles frowned with her mouth but smiled with her eyes. "Any further questions of this witness?"

"No."

"Does the prosecution wish to question this witness further?"

"No, Your Honor."

"The witness may step down, with the thanks of the court."

Two more morning witnesses testified that Ernie was not looking where he was going when he hit the bicycle. One was a ninety-year-old woman who crossed the room slowly with the help of a walker. She had been waiting outside her apartment for her nephew to pick her up when she saw the accident, she testified. Her mind was sharp and her memory detailed, but Jim was able to call into question her eyesight. "Ma'am, according to vehicle records, you had a drivers license until last year. Is that correct?"

"Yes." The witness beamed with pride. "Didn't use it much, but kept it up to date just in case. You never know."

"That's admirable. May I ask why you allowed the license to lapse?" Jim had done his homework and already knew the answer.

"I had no choice. They made me."

"The Department of Motor Vehicles wouldn't renew your license?"

"That's correct."

"Why on earth would they do that to a gentle woman like you?"

"The Commonwealth said I flunked the vision test. Can you believe that? Fifty years behind the wheel without an accident or even a moving violation. But they said I had to give up my license. Some people have no respect."

The second collaborating witness was a contractor on his way to a renovation job. He was just passing Ernie in the opposite direction when the accident occurred.

"Did you get a good look at what happened, or did you see it out of the corner of your eye?" Ted Conover asked the witness.

"Not out of the corner of my eye, no, sir. I glanced over as I passed because the pickup seemed to turn without regard for the traffic. It didn't appear to me that the driver was looking where he was going."

"Could you be more specific?"

"I can't swear to this but he appeared to be concentrating on something inside the car, in his lap perhaps."

Jim's cross-examination was brief. "You said, 'it didn't appear to me' and 'I can't swear to this.' Keep in mind that the defendant could face a prison sentence. Are you confident enough of what you saw that you could live with yourself if your testimony puts the defendant in prison?"

The witness hesitated. "If mine were the only testimony, no. But I assume there is other evidence to support the charge, otherwise there wouldn't be a trial."

"Thank you for your legal analysis, sir. No further questions."

A middle-aged couple had attended every day of the trial. On his way out of the courtroom at lunchtime, Jim passed the couple and the man halted him. He had a hardened face belied by a tailored suit. "Sir, we're the Degregorios. Our son Vinnie, Jr. was the young man your client killed."

"I'm terribly sorry for your loss."

"Why would a man of your reputation take this case?"

Jim was startled by the question. Never had this happened to him in his years on the bench. And the father looked smart enough to know better. "We really can't be talking. If you'll excuse me."

Degregorio stopped Jim by the arm. "We're watching you."

Jim shook him off. "Are you threatening me, sir?"

Mrs. Degregorio spoke. "Oh, no, not threatening you, judge. We're expressing our concern, that's all. You can understand why. Our son had such a bright future."

The woman looked saddened, sincere, downtrodden. Jim believed she meant well. He acknowledged that with a respectful nod. "We're all concerned that justice be done here, ma'am."

"Please don't mind my husband. He's very upset."

The man bared his teeth. Upset, indeed. Apoplectic?

"I understand." Jim left the couple and walked out into the sunshine. He had to report this incident. He pulled Ted aside before the afternoon session and told him what happened.

"Do you want me to speak to the parents? They're not bad people, just distraught," Ted said.

"No, I just want you to know it won't change the way I represent my client."

Ted nodded. "I can't imagine you being intimidated."

"Pissed, is more like it."

"I hope to wrap up my case this afternoon. If all goes well, I'll turn it over to you tomorrow."

"I'll be ready."

6

The prosecution rested its case before day's end, and Pat Knowles recessed for the night. Jim had one more night to decide whether to put Ernie on the witness stand in his own defense. The burden to prove guilt is always on the prosecution – a defendant has no obligation to testify, nor does the defense have an obligation to present evidence if the prosecution has failed to prove its case.

Jim thought the case against Ernie weak. The forensic evidence did not in and of itself establish negligence or that Ernie had been texting at the time of the accident, and Jim thought he had done a good job poking holes in the eyewitness testimony. In Jim's opinion, the Commonwealth had failed to prove its case, and he thought that Pat Knowles – a stickler for evidence – would agree. Putting Ernie on the stand would gain little and there was a real chance he would blow it. If any disdain showed through, if even the tiniest hint of a sneer tugged the corners of Ernie's mouth, Pat Knowles would notice and the weakness of the case against Ernie could be turned in the prosecution's favor. Pascal said 'can't hurt, might help,' when asked why he believed in God. Putting Ernie Farrell on the witness stand wouldn't help, might hurt. Jim took his decision to bed with him. It was a big gamble. Sleep might change his mind.

He got up early the next morning and took a bus to the courthouse, arriving well before time for the trial. He sat with a cup of coffee and a cranberry muffin at a nearby sandwich shop and tried to imagine what would run through Pat Knowles's head if the defense rested. Same conclusion as the night before. Not worth the risk to put Ernie on the stand. Sleep had not changed his mind.

Jim arrived at the courtroom twenty minutes early. A scruffy-looking man sat by himself in the back row. Jim fleetingly wondered why the man had chosen the back row when he had most of the courtroom to himself. Something about him put Jim on high alert, maybe his close-set eyes and fixed stare: the stare of a madman. Jim thought: I saw plenty of stray people in my courtroom. They came to get out of cold or to have something to do. Some of them became quite knowledgeable about courtroom proceedings. So why does this man rattle me so? He looks vaguely familiar. Did he appear before me when I was a judge? Why is he staring at me like that?

"Mornin," Jim said to Ernie, who was already at the defense table.

Ernie leaned toward Jim, his face a fighter's. "I'm ready, as ready as I'll ever be."

"I'm not putting you on the witness stand."

Ernie snapped backwards so hard he almost knocked his chair over. "What are you talking about?"

"The burden is on the prosecution to prove your guilt. It hasn't. Putting you on the stand would gain nothing and opens you up to a withering cross-examination by Ted Conover, and I can't be sure you won't revert to being a wise-guy."

Ernie almost head-butted Jim. "Let me get this straight. You're not going to let me testify?"

"Correct. I'm going to rest the case."

Ernie flung his hands towards the sky. "I'm cooked."

"You wanted me to be your lawyer. Judge Knowles is a stickler for evidence, and not enough evidence has been presented to prove guilt. Under the law you are innocent until proven guilty. You have the right to dismiss me and do what you originally were going to do, represent yourself. Otherwise, we do what I say."

Ernie looked over his shoulder at Janet, dismay cleaving his face. But there was no time for Janet to react because the bailiff cried, "All rise," and Patricia Knowles sailed into the courtroom and mounted the bench.

"Are counsel ready to proceed?"

"The prosecution is ready, Your Honor."

Jim rose. "The defense is ready, Your Honor."

"Judge Randall, you may proceed."

"Thank you, Your Honor. The defense rests and moves to dismiss based on a lack of sufficient evidence to prove the charges."

The courtroom stirred. Judge Knowles seemed unsurprised. She banged her gavel for calm. "Mr. Conover?"

Ted rose slowly to his feet. He glanced at Jim, no surprise showing, then calmly addressed the court. "Prosecution rests, Your Honor."

"Both sides having rested and a motion for dismissal having been made, I shall now recess to consider my decision. I urge no one to stray very far." She rose and departed through the back door, taking the energy in the courtroom with her.

"What now?" Ernie said.

"We wait."

Behind them Janet was on her feet and red in the face. "What are you doing?" she hissed at Jim.

Jim stood and faced her. "It's for the best."

"You have just sent my husband to jail."

"No, I haven't. Wait and see. I'm betting the case will be thrown out. If you'll excuse me, I'm going to wait in the hall."

As he exited the courtroom he noted that the menacing man in the back row was gone, his absence as jarring as his fixed stare. Who was he? Jim was sure he had seen him before.

At the far end of the hallway Jim spotted the Degregorios. They were the last people he wanted to encounter. He turned and headed back into the courtroom, almost bumping into Ernie. "Janet's bullshit."

"I could tell," Jim replied.

"I just want you to know that whatever happens, I realize you're on my side, unlike my dad. I don't understand why you rested the case, but I know you're doing what you think is best."

Under the stressful circumstances that simple statement touched Jim and made him remember why he believed from the very beginning that he understood this kid. He laid his hand on Ernie's shoulder. "Thanks. We'd better go back in."

They didn't have long to wait. Judge Knowles entered and took her seat. "Everybody ready? I understand the strong emotions aroused by the death of a promising young man and I understand the desire of the Commonwealth to set an example of the consequences of texting while driving, but emotion and the desire to set an example are not sufficient to prove a crime. Negligence in the legal sense requires a greater degree of proof than the sense of the word in everyday life. If the defendant were on trial for a misdemeanor, the standard of proof would be easier to meet. In the case of *Commonwealth v Farrell*, the court concludes that the prosecution has failed to present sufficient evidence of negligence to prove a felony, and all charges against the defendant are dropped." She paused a beat before banging her gavel. "Court is adjourned." She stood and for the last time swept out of the courtroom, robe flying.

Ernie was on his feet, a look of shock on his face, his quivering voice that of a boy. "I'm free to go?"

Jim nodded. "You are." He turned when he felt someone approach. It was Janet, who hugged Ernie and wept.

Ernie hugged her for a minute then pried her away. "Let's go home. We have to talk."

Before they left, Janet hugged Jim. "Thank you. I'm sorry I doubted you."

"You've both been under a lot of stress. It's over. Be good to each other."

Jim lingered after the Farrells had gone and the courtroom had emptied, collecting his thoughts. Courtrooms felt like home, no matter which side of the bench he was on, and he was reluctant to leave.

He finally turned to go. Blocking the door were the Degregorios. Jim grimaced and tried to pass.

"Just a minute," the father said, grabbing Jim's arm.

"Take your hands off me, sir. I am sorry for the loss of your son, but justice was served today."

"You haven't heard the last of this," the father spat. "Mark my words."

Jim remained calm. "Get out of my way, Mr. Degregorio."

The man glared, then dropped Jim's arm. "You can go, but mark my words. You haven't heard the last of this."

7

Rattled but elated, Jim longed for a woman to share his victory with. Someone who would understand what the win meant for him. Someone with whom he wouldn't have to fill in the blanks, who understood the shorthand of married speech.

In lieu of a woman, he went to Vermont.

The first day he couldn't shake the muscle memory of Degregorio grabbing his bicep, growing angrier and angrier each time he remembered. Furious, ready to fight. He knew how to remain calm when he had to be calm but blew his cool when bullied. Same thing with impulsiveness: level-headed 95% of the time, impulsive 5% (but never while on the bench). He told himself to put himself in Degregorio's shoes and think of how he would feel. Your son is dead and the man you blame for his death gets off – you'd be as aggrieved as Degregorio. By dinnertime, Jim had relaxed enough to savor his victory. Ernie had won, *he* had won.

To celebrate, he took himself to the closest fancy restaurant (fancy meaning white tablecloths) and treated himself to a profiterole with vanilla ice cream and hot fudge sauce for desert, thereby blowing months of careful eating. When I go wild, Judge Randall said to his imaginary companion for the night – an attractive, younger woman – I go hog-wild.

After the drive home through a typically dark Vermont night (when Jim was in Cambridge he forgot how dark Vermont nights were), he felt like an adulterer, having shared dinner with a make-believe woman who wasn't Joyce. The imposter hadn't even liked the food.

He slept well and the next morning, Ted Conover called to congratulate him. "Your rust didn't show, my friend."

"What rust?"

Ted chuckled. "Seriously, nice job. If you quote me on this, I'll call you a liar, but I have rarely been on the receiving end of such intense political pressure to throw the book at someone. Your client messed up, but the victim's father is generous with campaign contributions. I believe you when you say he threatened you, but he is much beloved, a real pillar of his community. And the pols who took campaign contributions from Ernie Farrell's father still seethe at having their names tainted when he went to jail. Talk about a rock and a hard place."

"So you knew the case was questionable but you prosecuted it anyway?"

"Don't put it like that. My job is always a balancing act between politics and justice. I had to bring serious charges or face the wrath of a bunch of pols who fund our office, but I hated the thought of young Farrell representing himself. That's why I asked your opinion about how to change his mind."

"Tell me the truth. When you asked me, did you hope I'd represent him?"

"I do not have that good an imagination. No, I just wanted the benefit of your advice. But I was glad when you took the case. You did the right thing by resting the case when you did. A lawyer who didn't know how judges think might have lacked the nerve."

"I don't know how you can stomach the politics of your job. I couldn't."

"Oh, there are compensations. I've put lots of bad guys away and in the end, young Farrell got a fair trial. Did being back in the courtroom whet your appetite?"

"To litigate more cases? No, this was a special situation. Did I tell you that after the trial Degregorio delivered another none-too-subtle threat to me?"

"Really?"

"Do you think he's dangerous?"

"No, distraught but not dangerous. But maybe I don't know him as well as I think I do."

Jim was startled by the sound of a key turning in the front door lock. A moment later, Casey Allen entered, carrying her vacuum cleaner. She stopped abruptly when she saw Jim.

"You surprised me, Judge. I didn't know you were here."

"Sorry. Came up on the spur of the moment. I should've let you and Jake know."

"No problem. Do you want me to come back later? I don't mind."

"No, stay. You won't bother me."

He had brought a sheaf of papers with him, thinking to catch up on bills and paperwork, and had the papers spread out over the dinner table in the main room. He liked to work by the window because it overlooked the river valley and because it got good sun in the morning. As he sat down to work, he knew he was delaying the inevitable – the moment when he would have caught up on his paperwork and have nothing to do.

He heard water running in the kitchen. He tried to imagine Casey as Joyce but couldn't. Joyce never cleaned floors, as he could hear Casey doing. Joyce would rather die than pick up a mop. Manual labor of other kinds was fine, but mops remained her bête noire. He never found out why.

He fiddled with his papers, took his reading glasses on and off for effect, looked at the sun and tried to feel pleasure from his victory, then blurted, "What the hell, I'm bored out of my skull."

He went to the kitchen – not a great distance in the small house – ostensibly to refill his coffee cup but mainly for company. Casey was busy wet mopping. "Watch your step, Jim," she warned him.

Sometimes she called him Jim, sometimes Judge. He had tried without success to figure out which she used when; if there were an inflection point, he couldn't discern it.

He leaned against the counter, coffee cup in hand, and crossed his ankles – nonchalance personified. "How's it going?"

Casey straightened up and wiped her brow with the back of her hand. "Oh, very well. Keeping busy, you know."

"You like that, don't you?"

She had an athlete's build. "It's why I pitch in to help Jake. We both love to keep busy."

"Good for you." Jim pushed off from the counter. "Knowing what's right for you is important."

She narrowed her pale blue-with-a-hint-of-something eyes. "Did I read that you just tried a case?"

"Yes. Vehicular homicide. Young man on a bike."''

"That's it! BostonGlobe.com, wasn't it?"

"Yes, I believe they reported it."

"I don't get it, I thought you stopped being a judge."

"Once a lawyer, always a lawyer. But you're right, I'm retired. I tried the case on a whim."

"How did it go?"

"I won but take little credit."

"Why?"

He liked Casey's directness. No blurring of questions, no worries about how they would be received, and most importantly, no thought given to the status of who she was asking. Very Vermont.

"The case against my client was weak. I enjoyed the trial, but it was nerve-wracking. I'm more of the contemplative type, at my best with a book or a gavel."

Casey resumed mopping. "Me too, although you wouldn't know it to look at me."

Jim hesitated a moment, thinking about what she said, then went into the living room and picked up where he left off – which was wondering what he was going to do after he finished catching up on his paperwork. To kill time, he speculated on why he identified with a young man with a sneer on his face who hadn't lived up to his potential. Jim had been a favorite of his mother and his teachers, studious, never in trouble, good at playing by himself. But his father – his father's attitude towards him was a different story.

My Dad – someday I should write his story, Jim mused. A man who had a hunger for affirmation without the drive to achieve it. A man who wouldn't let Jim love him, a man who wanted the best for his son but failed to understand him. He had hoped Jim would join him in at least one of his failed business ventures. Instead, Jim went to law school. His dad died bitter, broke. Jim's mother, a wonderful woman and usually Jim's biggest cheerleader, had blamed him: "If you had helped your dad more, he might still be alive" – her one flaw being her inability to see her husband for who he truly was.

Ernie Farrell had rebelled against his upbringing by underachieving. Jim rebelled by becoming obsessed with injustice.

He stood to shake off the memories. Didn't work, so he sought out Casey. By the sound of her vacuum cleaner, she was in the bedroom.

She turned off the machine when she saw him coming.

"Sorry to interrupt, Casey. Have you seen my reading glasses?"

"The glasses on top of your head?"

"My second pair, I mean." He didn't have a second pair.

"No, I haven't. I'll let you know if I do."

"Never mind." He was making up things on the fly. He turned to go, then, "How are your kids?"

"Fine. I'm worried about the fourteen-year-old, though. She's catnip to boys. I warn her to be careful, but she laughs at me. 'Mom, I know all about sex.'"

Jim smiled. "You're right to warn her. Men are scum."

Casey smiled. "Judge! I'm shocked."

"It's probably good that Joyce and I didn't have kids. I'd have been an obnoxious father."

"I'll bet you would have been a great father."

Under the circumstances, that moved him. He felt lonely, very lonely. He blinked back tears. End of trial letdown. No, more than that.

Casey didn't notice. "Do you want me to vacuum the living room before you work?"

"Great. I'll watch."

"You can grab a mop, if you'd rather be helpful."

"I'm not that desperate for something to do."

She carried the vacuum cleaner into the living room. He followed. "The one thing my late wife would never do is mop. Dust, vacuum, yes, but Joyce wouldn't mop. I never figured out why."

Casey had turned on the vacuum cleaner and couldn't hear him. She turned it off and asked him to repeat what he said.

"My late wife wouldn't mop. Wouldn't touch a mop. You ever hear of mop phobia?"

"No, never. But I guess people are different." She restarted the vacuum cleaner. "Almost finished," she said over her shoulder. "Won't take a second."

He stepped outside to get some air. Vermont air had clarity, precision. He walked to the rear of the house and traced the sightline down the slope to the glint of the river. Beyond lay New Hampshire, where the air didn't measure up and the people were gun nuts.

Having filled his lungs with air and his spleen with enough bile to get him through the morning, and noticing through the window that Casey had finished vacuuming the living room, he went back in the house.

"All done, Judge," she said as he entered the room.

"Thanks." He stopped. "May I ask something that has intrigued me for a long time? Sometimes you call me Jim, sometimes judge. Any reason?"

"I hadn't really thought about it."

"No problem with either. I'm just curious."

"I guess it's sometimes you seem judge-like, sometimes Jim-like."

"Interesting."

Casey coiled the vacuum cleaner's cord. "If you don't mind my saying so, you need a wife. Have you ever come close to re-marrying?"

"No, not really. Haven't been particularly interested. Joyce spoiled me."

"I didn't know her well. She wouldn't let me. You're keeping me from my work, judge."

"Jim thanks you for the chat."

*

He drove back to Cambridge the next day, post-trial emptiness still acute. In the few days he had been gone, mail had accumulated on the vestibule floor. Bills, grocery store fliers, magazines – *Time, The Atlantic, The New Yorker.* A folded piece of lined paper caught his eye. He scooped it off the floor and unfolded it. The paper was wide-ruled, like grade school paper. Letters had been cut from newspapers and pasted awkwardly on the page. The visual effect was comical, the message was not: **YOU WILL PAY FOR WHAT YOU DID.**

He went to the phone and rang Ted. "I just got back from Vermont. Guess what awaited me?" He read the note out loud.

"Let me guess. You think the threat came from Vincent Degregorio."

"I do. He looked ready to explode when he threatened me in the courtroom."

"Are you sure it wasn't you who was ready to explode, Jim?"

"I was angry, for sure, but not as angry as he was."

"The note sounds too crude to be from Degregorio, if you ask me. Have you shown it to the police?"

"Not yet. I called you first."

"Call the police. They will try to track the sender."

Cambridge forensics reported a few days later that the sender of the note could not be identified. The paper was widely available, the cutout letters from a variety of sources. No fingerprints or other clues. The officer Jim spoke to said, "I suggest you install deadbolt locks on your doors and lower your window shades at night. Let us know if anything changes. In the meantime, we'll increase patrols in your neighborhood."

He called Ted Conover. "Forensics drew a blank. What can you tell me about Degregorio that I don't already know?"

"You're not going to do anything foolish, are you?"

"If the note's not from him, there's no harm in learning more. If the note is from him, I need to know everything I can about him."

"He's the founder of Degregorio Hardware, which started as one store in Revere and grew into the largest hardware chain in Southern New England. He comes from a broken family and was raised by his grandmother. He's rich and politically connected, generous with his money, but retains deep resentment at how the world looked down on him while he was growing up. He has been quoted in interviews as saying the only thing which saved him from a life on the margins was his own hard work. Has a daughter but no sons other than the one who died."

"Just a guess. Was he expecting his son to take over the business?"

"Probably, but I don't know that for a fact."

"Does he blame you for losing the case, or do I have the honor?"

"You have the honor."

To Jim's horror, Joyce did not join him at the dinner table that night. He needed to talk to her about the threatening note. What had he done to drive her away? Had she sensed his fear? Would she reappear?

She came to him when he was in bed, but dimly, as through a fog. "How was your day?" he thought he heard her say.

"Where did you go?" he demanded. "I've been frantic."

She disappeared before he could hear her answer.

He was working in his study the next morning when the doorbell rang. FedEx with a shoebox-size package, return address West Virginia. He started to unwrap it but stopped and called the police sergeant he had spoken to earlier.

"Is there a return address?"

"JG Distributing, Wheeling, West Virginia."

"Are you expecting anything from them?"

"Never heard of them."

"I take it you're worried what might be in the package and want us to test it."

"Because of the threat, yes. Would you mind?"

"I'll send a patrol car around to pick it up."

The sergeant reported back within an hour. "Did you recently order a pair of black shoes, size 12?"

"Yes."

"They've arrived. You can pick them up whenever you want."

8

He hid his chagrin that evening at Duck, Duck, Goose. The counter was full so he had to wait, and when he was seated, he wasn't tucked into his preferred spot at the corner of the counter but wedged between an intense young man and an attractive middle-aged woman.

"The usual, judge?" Chris said from behind the counter.

"I didn't know I had a usual."

"Anything French and red."

"Sounds good. Surprise me."

Chris hauled out a bottle and showed it to Jim. "We just got this. Languedoc-Rousillion. More Carignan than usual. Care to try it?"

"I'll be your guinea pig."

Chris opened the bottle and poured Jim a splash. He sniffed and sipped. "Not bad."

"Shall I fill your glass?"

"Why not?"

Jim glanced at the woman next to him. A good twenty years younger than him. Short hair, stylish clothes. She had a knowing smile on her face; he couldn't tell if it was her habitual expression or if she found the wine ritual amusing. He tipped his glass to her. "Cheers."

"Is it any good?"

"Very."

"I wish I liked wine better."

"Everyone likes wine once they know the difference between good wine and bad."

"My ex-husband, who's a jerk, liked wine too much which soured me on it."

"My late wife preferred whiskey, but she liked a glass of wine or two with dinner now and then."

The woman's food arrived. "Arlene," she told Jim before she dug in.

"Jim," Jim replied. "Nice to meet you."

Arlene read her phone while she ate. Jim was left to reflect on the pain in his big right toe caused by his new shoes, and the lingering unease caused by the threatening note. Chris handed him a menu, and he ordered chicken-under-a-brick and a second glass of wine. He didn't look forward to returning to an empty house, especially now that he couldn't count on Joyce to appear. He debated getting to know Arlene better but the truth was, he didn't want company. He didn't want to be lonely but he didn't want company.

Arlene finished her meal long before he did. As she paid her check she said, "Cheer up. Things will get better."

"Why do you say that? Do I look sad?"

"Very." She stood to go. "I was sad, too, so I know." She touched his shoulder. "Take care."

Jim didn't know what to make of that. He was startled, to say the least. *I guess I am sad, though not as sad as she apparently thinks.* Chris the counterman came over to ask if everything was all right. At first Jim thought he was picking up where Arlene left off, then realizing he was simply asking about the food. "Very good, as usual," Jim replied.

Chris gave the counter a two-handed pat before going to greet an arriving couple. Jim sometimes thought counter talk the ideal kind of conversation: impersonal, short, predictable.

Jim was a light eater. Chris stopped by again when Jim had eaten all he wanted. "Finished, Judge?"

"I am."

"Want me to wrap that?"

"No. That won't be necessary."

The short walk home did him good. The air was stale compared to Vermont, but at least it was open air. Cambridge air was a little like Cambridge itself, stuffy, slightly pretentious, but mostly satisfying.

He turned on the light and went to the mantel to look at his favorite photo of Joyce, taken shortly after they married. In it, she was smiling without inhibition, her face tilted towards the sun. Her smile in later life was guarded so he especially treasured this portrait.

Something mildly disturbed him. A nuance. He called his sister, Natalie, in Oregon. "I'm beginning to think about women."

"It's about time," Natalie answered. "It's been what? Twelve years?"

"Thirteen."

"Anyone in particular?"

"No. It's just that now when I talk to women, I notice that they are women."

"An attractive man, old enough to be safe but not old enough to be out of commission, notices women as women? You lech."

"Don't mock me. This is disturbing for me."

"Sorry, Jim. I'm not mocking. Joyce was a lucky woman to have you. Of course the flip side is you are one of the most set-in-your-ways men I have ever known and maybe your posthumous devotion to Joyce is more a matter of habit than devotion." Natalie had a lilt in her voice that made everything, even criticism, sound like a caress.

"Wash your mouth out. Speaking of devotion, how's Stuart?"

"It's hard, Jim. His decline is so slow I hardly notice until the signs accumulate, then his deterioration staggers me. I know we're all going to die, but to lose yourself before you go seems unspeakably cruel and unjust."

"Justice is a human invention."

"Is that supposed to make me feel better?"

"I love you, little sister, pain in the ass though you are. I'll be glad to fly out and stay with Stuart for a few days if you need to get away. You have to take care of yourself."

"Not necessary yet. Maybe later, that would be great. We're coping okay now."

"Let me know."

She shifted gears. "I didn't mean to get off the subject. You called for romantic advice. My advice is go for it."

"Okay. First I have to find a woman."

"That would be an advisable first step."

Next morning, to have the company of strangers, he took himself to The Long Gone. Drinking his coffee he wondered how Ernie was doing post-trial. Did his father rejoice that the charges against Ernie had been dropped? Jim doubted it; he probably demanded to know why Ernie had gotten himself into the mess in the first place. Jim wondered if Ernie's father and Vincent Degregorio had ever crossed paths. They would probably find they had much in common.

The barista sounded like a town crier as he shouted each drink and the name of the person who ordered it. Hunched over laptops, plugged into phones, no one took note.

A voicemail was waiting when Jim got home: Ernie, sounding panicked – Vincent Degregorio had filed a civil suit seeking damages for his son's death.

"I have no money, what is he trying to do?" Ernie demanded when Jim returned the call.

"Ruin you. He'll seek to garnish your wages for the rest of your life."

"Can he win?"

"The standard of proof is lower in civil suits than in criminal cases. He has a better chance."

"Will you represent me? *Please?*"

"No, I'm sorry, I've done all I can. You need a lawyer who's experienced in civil suits. Someone who knows how to negotiate a settlement, which is how suits for damages usually end. I can't do a good job for you."

"Don't let me down."

"Ernie, I did what I could to help you. This is not for me."

*

Judges learn not to second guess themselves, lest they go nuts; that doesn't mean they don't ever lapse. Should I have taken Ernie's civil case? preoccupied Jim for days. That worry vied with a personal concern: now that he noticed women, how to stop thinking about them? It was not so much a hormonal thing as a loneliness thing. Strange how the need for female companionship doesn't ebb even though the testosterone level does. Maybe Plato had it right: man and woman, now two, yearn to return to their primeval state as one.

He was preoccupied with both worries a few evenings later as he lingered over the newspaper and a glass of wine at home. His legs were crossed in an awkward way and his reading glasses kept slipping down his nose. On TV the news was bad, horrible, couldn't be worse, the doomsday intonation of the announcers not helping; more after this word from our sponsor – don't take our pills if you've ever had problems with your liver, kidneys, or skin, if you prefer coffee to tea, if you've ever known a left-handed person. He knocked over his wine glass as he reached for it. The world, my knees, my failing coordination, woe is me. Wine spilled over the edge of the table onto the floor.

He sighed and fetched a dishrag to wipe up the mess.

On his hands and knees beneath the table. An announcer's voice on TV – "In local news, Vincent Degregorio has filed a civil suit against Ernie Farrell seeking ten million dollars in damages for the wrongful death of his son, Vincent, Jr."

Jim bumped his head against the underside of the table at the magnitude of the requested damages. Maybe it wasn't too late. Call Ernie and offer my services. But he was a little drunk, in no shape to make decisions. He tossed the wine-dark dishrag into the sink and went to his study to read Homer.

By the morning, he had a plan. "Meet me at The Long Gone and I'll explain," he said to Ernie over the phone.

Ernie looked the same. "Have you changed your mind about representing me? Is that why you wanted to meet? Please say yes."

"No, but here's what I can offer. I won't be your attorney of record, meaning I won't argue your case in court or file motions on your behalf, but I can be an informal adviser to you and your attorney. Have you hired one yet?"

"All I can afford is a guy I know from high school. He's a solo practitioner who does mostly real estate but said he'd take my case for the experience."

"Is he any good?"

"I don't know. Smart guy when I knew him in school."

"Talk to him. Ask him how he feels about an informal collaboration. I would be 'of counsel' to him. That's all I can offer."

*

Jim's legal juices were now flowing. If Ernie accepted his offer, he needed to be prepared. He drove to his house in Vermont to think. Casey was mopping when he arrived.

"How are you?" he asked, tired from the two-and-a-half hour drive.

"Fine, Jim. Watch your step. Floor's wet."

"As I see. I'll be here a few days."

He kept a backup of essentials – clothes, books, laptop – in Vermont so he wouldn't have to lug them back and forth. The idea was to be able to move from one house to the other without a lot of thought. Throw whatever he was reading into a tote bag and go.

He deposited his bag in the bedroom and stretched out on the bed to unkink his joints, which had stiffened up on the drive. He could hear Casey bustling about in the living room. Clasping his hands behind his head, he closed his eyes and drifted off.

Casey's soft voice woke him. "Jim, I'm leaving." He opened his eyes. She had materialized in the bedroom door. "Sorry. The door was open. Didn't mean to wake you."

He bolted upright. "Just dozing. You're off?"

"Yes."

"How long have you and Jake been married?"

"Eighteen years. Judge, you're lonely. Find a woman to be with. I can't imagine you staying alone for the rest of your life."

"Easier said than done."

"There are a lot more widows than widowers. You're a catch."

"A catch?"

"Stop fishing for compliments, Jim."

"Why?"

She chuckled. "You'd probably stand a better chance if you took steps to meet women. Have you tried online dating?"

"Wash your mouth out. Me?"

"You could try and see what happens."

"Not a chance." He scoffed as only he could scoff.

Her voice softened. She checked the time. "I have to go, Jim. I've got two more houses to do."

He stood. "Of course. I'm grateful to you for humoring me. Jake's a lucky man." He enlarged his voice. "The witness may step down from the witness stand and is free to leave, with the thanks of the court."

"Do I need to enter the witness protection program, Your Honor?"

"Won't be necessary. You may go."

He felt refreshed when she left. He fixed himself a sandwich, then sat down with his laptop. Was the civil suit a bargaining chip or pure revenge? From what Jim could learn online, Degregorio was philanthropic, egotistical, crude and charming in equal measure – one file photo showed Degregorio looking like an extra in The Sopranos, another showed him in black tie at a charity event. The testimonials to him for his philanthropic work – the Degregorio Pediatric Wing at Suffolk Community Hospital, the annual Vincent T. Degregorio Golf Tournament to support lymphoma research, and the newly founded scholarship fund named in memory of his deceased son, the Vincent Degregorio, Jr. Scholarship Fund – were glowing.

Light from the valley obscured the screen of Jim's laptop. He switched seats so he could work glare-free.

*

Loneliness felled him like the flu when he was back in Cambridge. Was there any reason other than pride why he shouldn't try online dating, as Casey had suggested? You are a lawyer, think like one. Is there any reason not to at least try?

But damn if he would capitulate to a dating site for seniors. 'Retired widower with creaky knees and a bad disposition seeks a female companion content with an emotional tightwad.' He searched various sites and found one aimed at 'never too late singles.' Hold your nose and just do it. Okay, here goes: he registered, spent less than twenty minutes drafting his plea, and posted it before he came to his senses. To his shock and surprise he got ten replies almost immediately, which scared the hell out of him.

He sorted through the replies and picked out two that seemed reasonable. A widow in her fifties with two grown children, and a sixty-three-year-old woman who was proud of never marrying. A little *too* proud, he decided upon reflection, and he responded only to the first woman, suggesting they meet for a drink in Harvard Square. Conveniently she lived on the Red Line.

They agreed to meet on a Wednesday, as neutral a day as one can find: a middle of the week, neither here nor there day. The agonies of the damned took on new meaning as the date approached, what to wear presenting a tougher choice than guilty or not guilty. No tie, no one wore a tie in Cambridge. His tweed jacket and a turtleneck? No, turtlenecks had been out for decades; be ashamed for even thinking of a turtleneck. His tweed jacket and an open-necked French blue shirt? Done.

He looked in a mirror. Dead man in tweed. What a terrible idea this was!

But he had told this woman – whose name was Harriet Malcolm – he would come, and he was a man of his word.

Harriet was already at the Basement in Harvard Square when he arrived. She stood when she saw him as if someone had shouted, all rise! How did she know I was a judge? he wondered, then realized she was just being polite.

"Hi." He extended his hand. "I'm Jim."

"I could tell." Harriet shook hands and sat back down.

She was an attractive woman who dressed with care. He had the impression of a quietly controlled woman, a guarded woman who welcomed opportunities to be less guarded. He got that impression from her careful smile, her quick handshake, and the fluid way she moved. Another reason he preferred women: men didn't give off subtle signals, women did; women were cursive, men were block letters.

"I have never done this before, and I don't know where to begin," Jim began.

"The beginning is always awkward, don't worry."

"You've done this before?"

She nodded. "Three or four times. Nice men, none a match."

Jim leaned forward far enough to cross his arms, thought better of it, and leaned back. Which made him conscious of his hands, and he suddenly didn't know what to do with them. He kept one on the table and rested the other in his lap. Nonchalant – he thought. Very nonchalant. I was never this uncomfortable on the bench.

Because he could think of absolutely nothing else to say, he asked, "how did you know it was me when I came in?"

Harriet's eyes had the glint of someone who liked to be amused by life. "By your look of abject terror."

"I'm embarrassed."

"Don't be. Here's a good place to start – what kind of work did you retire from?"

"I was a judge."

She leaned back to get a better look. "I can see it. Yes, definitely."

"And you? What did you do?"

"Still do. Middle-school principal."

"That must be more challenging than being a judge."

She disagreed. "Judging guilt or innocence strikes me as much harder than what I do."

"Depends on one's temperament. I don't mind making judgements about other people. Knowing myself is what I avoid."

"But sending people to prison?"

"A lot of people deserve it, believe me. There are some bad actors out there."

"Did you ever worry about making mistakes?"

"Early in my career I agonized over every decision. Joyce, my late wife, used to lose patience. But I got good at deciding."

"Tell me about her."

"A woman of sound mind, occasionally ornery, kept to herself a lot, generous to her friends. If I had been born a woman, I'd hope to be like her."

"That's the highest compliment a man can give a woman."

"Really?"

"You have been out of touch with women, haven't you?"

"Joyce died thirteen years ago, and this is the first time I've seriously thought of dating. I hate that word."

"How did she die?"

"Painfully. Can we not talk about this?"

"Sorry. Then let me tell you about my Jim."

"Your late husband's name was Jim, too? That's creepy."

"Yes, I know. He died six years ago of pancreatic cancer. A surgeon, a healer."

"I'm sorry," Jim said. He fidgeted. "Another drink?"

The bar was a basement bar for serious talkers. The talk was mostly academic in nature: overcast with scattered showers.

"Love to." She smiled.

Jim stopped a waitperson (three syllables), who happened to be a waiter (two syllables). To be PC in Cambridge you have to be multi-syllabic.

"Another martini for the lady."

"Excellent. And another glass of wine for you, sir?" the waitperson said.

"Not now. Maybe we'll have something to eat." Jim glanced at Harriet to see her reaction, which was mildly amused.

"Very good, sir. I'll bring menus."

Jim turned to Harriet. "Was he supercilious or was it my imagination?"

"Your imagination. A dating tip for the future. Don't say another martini for the lady."

"Why not?"

"Haven't you heard? Women don't like to be called ladies anymore."

"Why on earth not?"

"You have been out of touch, haven't you?"

"Can I say another martini for my date person?"

She laughed. A bright, crystalline laugh. The rest of the evening was pleasant. She seemed to have a good time, and so did he.

"Shall I walk you to the Red Line?" he asked after they had a bite to eat.

"How romantic."

"I am incurably romantic, Red Line, Blue Line. I'll walk a woman to any line."

At the subway entrance, she offered her hand. "Thank you, Jim number two. You are very nice."

"Shall we do this again?"

"I'd like to, but why don't you think it over? You may need another thirteen years."

That stung a little, but he had survived with limbs intact, and walked home pleased with himself.

She was nice, he thought once inside his sanctuary. That was enough of a step forward for now.

He went to the living room and asked the picture of Joyce he kept on the mantle if she were okay with what he had done. She seemed impatient. "Okay with it?" he imagined her saying. "What took you so long?"

9

Cambridge Street was buzzing and humming with traffic as Jim walked to The Long Gone. A school bus barreled up the street towards the high school. A sullen young man stared out the window – at me, Jim imagined. A van screeched to a stop at the curb next to Jim. Jim flinched, then watched the driver lift a vase of flowers from the rear of the van and hurry into Cambridge Hospital.

He reached The Long Gone before Ernie. Ernie walked in twenty minutes late, very apologetic. "I'm so sorry." He dropped his backpack at the table and ordered at the counter.

"You look furious," Jim said when Ernie returned to the table.

"Dad is driving me fuckin' nuts. I called him as a courtesy – big mistake, the civil suit has reawakened his demons. The family name dragged through the mud, and all that crap."

"How's your young lawyer?"

"Alex is clueless but he's fuckin' smart."

"And we are going to avoid saying fuckin' in court, correct?"

"Sorry. Sorry. My nerve endings are frayed."

"You are not alone. Now, let's review where you stand."

For the next twenty minutes – interrupted only by Ernie picking up his café mocha at the counter when his name was shouted – Ernie and Jim talked strategy. At the end Jim said, "Alex sounds smart, as you say, but you need a more experienced lawyer. Won't your dad help you with the cost?"

"No way in hell would I let him, if he offered, which he hasn't and won't. Judge, you don't understand. Dad is about facades – loving husband and family man, virtuous children, successful business. I crack the facade."

"Has he been like this your whole life?"

"Pretty much so. At least that's how I remember him. Janet says I overreact."

Jim leaned forward and spoke softly. "We are not so different, you and I. While my father was alive, he couldn't find much good in me. I never measured up, even when I became a judge. It took a long time, but I finally realized he was jealous of my accomplishments and had to run them down to save face. When I realized that, I came to terms with a simple truth: he wasn't the father I wanted, but he was the father I had. You haven't reached that acceptance yet."

Ernie started to speak but Jim stopped him. "I'm not finished. A mismatch between father and son is commonplace. You haven't been singled out for unusual punishment."

Ernie looked stunned. "No one's ever talked to me like this before."

Jim smiled. "I used to pass judgement for a living."

*

Duck, Duck, Goose for an early dinner. Chris behind the bar looked forlorn. "Am I the first?" Jim said, taking his usual seat at the elbow of the counter. "I guess I am," he answered his own question.

Chris gave Jim a splash of Madiran to try.

"Too dense," Jim passed judgement. He thought he had gotten through to Ernie today, and he felt good about that. "Like me."

"I'll bring you something lighter." Chris went to the row of bottles he kept for wines by the glass, poured a glass, and carried it to Jim. "Loire. Not your favorite, but I think you'll like this. Fruity without being sweet."

"Like me in my better days." Jim tipped his glass to Chris. "A question. Did you notice the woman I chatted up a week ago?"

"Dark hair, attractive, ignored you and read?"

"That's her. Had you seen her before? Do you know anything about her?"

Chris shook his head. "First time. Why, are you interested?"

"Curious, that's all."

"Want me to keep an eye out?"

"If you can do so discretely."

"Bartenders are as discrete as judges. I tell each customer only what they like to hear. You're looking young tonight, Judge."

"How kind."

"Decided on what you want to eat?"

"Something good for a change."

Why does my house keep getting bigger? Jim asked himself when he was back in his townhouse. Age compresses time but can it alter one's spatial sense? Another question:

what difference does it make whether Ernie comes to terms with his father? And why has my mood suddenly plummeted?

He went to bed without answers, knowing only that he was tired of being alone.

A week went by. Ernie's young lawyer didn't call Jim for advice. Jim was bored. When he called Natalie to complain, she was unsympathetic. "You're healthy, you're solvent. If you're bored, do volunteer work."

"Volunteer work doesn't appeal to me."

"Why not?"

"Too fleeting, too insubstantial."

"My brother is a crank and an ingrate."

"I take offense. I am a curmudgeon and a grouse, but not a crank and an ingrate."

"What's going on, Jim? Why did you really call? It wasn't to complain about too much free time."

"I hate it when I can't fool you. I don't want to be an open book."

"Oh, yes, you do. More than anything you do. Out with it, why did you call?"

"Something is going on inside me, and I can't figure it out. Maybe the threatening note is spooking me more than I realize."

"What threatening note?"

"Didn't I tell you?"

"Noooo. Maybe you should."

"An anonymous note stuck under my door.'"

"Good Lord! Did you tell the police?'

"They couldn't trace it. I assume it's from Vincent Degregorio, the father of the college student who died."

"Why would he threaten you if he's going to file a civil suit?"

"I don't know. Stop asking questions."

"What don't you go to Vermont for a while? Get away from threats and courts."

"I was just there. It didn't help. Something big is going to happen, and it'll happen here."

When he hung up it was Saturday noon Natalie-time, mid-afternoon in Cambridge and he called Harriet Malcolm before he gave himself time to think. She sounded tentative, as if by answering the phone on a Saturday afternoon she was letting an intruder into her life.

"Harriet, this is Jim Randall. From the other night?"

"Hello, Jim. How are you?"

He exhaled. "I'm fine. Listen, I was wondering if you'd like to have dinner with me tonight. Sorry I'm calling at the last minute. You probably have plans."

He detected amusement in her voice. "Correct, I have dozens of dinner invitations, fifty-something widows being in high demand. I'd love to have dinner with you tonight."

"Wonderful. Do you know Duck, Duck, Goose?"

Jim called Bruce as soon as he hung up and requested a table for two.

"We're actually full, but for you, Judge, we have a table."

Jim did not suffer the agony of the damned this time as he dressed for dinner. Second time's the charm, he told himself. He dressed casually, blazer, khakis, no tie of course. If he showed up at Duck, Duck, Goose with a tie, Bruce would refuse him the table.

Harriet arrived by cab. She looked elegant. "Did you bring your gavel?" she asked as they were seated. Jim so often ate at the counter and so seldom at a table that he felt out of place – altered spatial sense again. Settle down; relax; enjoy. Easier said than done, but as the evening progressed, Jim managed to do all three. Harriet was delightful company; attentive, observational, insightful. He wasn't drawn to her physically, but maybe with time.

The thought rattled Jim, made him seize up.

Harriet noticed. "What's wrong?"

"Nothing. Nothing at all."

"Did you have a good poker face on the bench?"

"I believe so. Why do you ask?"

"Because your face is a billboard tonight."

"Good lord, you've thoroughly spooked me."

She reached across the table and covered his hand. A school principal's reassuring touch. "It's nice. I like a man who shows his emotions." Job done, she withdrew her hand.

She talked about life as a middle school principal, he talked about life as a judge. They told amusing stories about their spouses. An enjoyable evening.

He felt emboldened. As Bruce fetched their coats, Jim asked Harriet if she'd care to stop by his house for an after-dinner drink. "I live just around the corner." He waved in the approximate direction of his house.

"By all means."

"Really?"

"The billboard again. Yes, Jim."

They didn't speak on the short walk, a walk which usually felt familiar but tonight felt new. He barely knew this woman, why in god's name were they going to his house?

He switched on the lights when they got there. He had not changed the look of the living room since Joyce died. Some of the furniture was new, but what hung on the walls was hers: color field paintings, family photos. Old and new, jumbled together. Joyce.

Jim helped Harriet off with her coat as she surveyed the room.

"I like it," she said, doing a 360.

"Joyce's doing."

"Is that her?" Harriet pointed to the photo on the mantle, his favorite photo of her.

"Yes," Jim murmured.

Harriet approached the mantle with care. She stared at the photo for a long time, saying nothing. She turned and smiled.

"Well? What's your reaction?" Jim asked.

"She doesn't look like I thought she would."

"How so?"

She looked at the photo again. "I thought she'd look formidable."

"Believe me, she was."

"But she looks childlike in the picture."

Jim recoiled. "Never have I heard that word used to describe Joyce. Even in moments of happiness she was not childlike."

Harriet turned away from the photo. "Would I have liked her if we met?"

"I doubt it." Jim went to the mantle to take a closer look. With a shock he realized he had not truly looked at this photo for thirteen years. Glanced at but not seen. The smiling woman in the photo was young, vibrant, on the verge of a giggle. As he gawked, wondering why he hadn't noted that before, the photo came to life and Joyce aged thirty years, grew gravely ill, became skin and bones, and stared at him from her deathbed. He gasped and shut his eyes.

"What's wrong? What happened?" Harriet asked in alarm.

"She's gone, isn't she?"

"Yes, Jim."

He shook his head. His eyes remained closed. "I hadn't looked closely."

She touched his arm. "Sweet Jim. I'd better leave. Another time."

He opened his eyes. "I'm really and truly sorry. I enjoy your company."

"Don't worry, I understand." She looked for her coat.

"I hung it in the closet. I'll get it." He helped her put it on. "I can drive you home."

"No, I'll take a cab."

"I'll walk you to the cab stand."

"That's not necessary, Jim. Stay here. You've had a shock."

"I'll call you."

He walked her to the door and held it open. "This is ridiculous. I'll walk you to the cab stand whether you want me to or not. Let me get my coat."

The walk to the cab stand was blessedly short. He knew he was stubborn, but thirteen years of denial? No one was that stubborn. Oh, yeah? As Harriet climbed in the cab, Jim leaned down to brush cheeks but was too late. "I'll call you," he said as he closed the door.

*

Jim and Ernie met Ernie's young lawyer for the first time later that week. The lawyer's name was Alec Mixner and the meeting took place in late afternoon in his small East Cambridge office, not far from the courthouse. Mixner looked young enough to be in high school.

"This is an honor, Judge. Your name still echoes in the courthouse."

"Actually, those are cries for my head," Jim said.

"As Ernie no doubt told you, I mostly handle purchase and sale agreements, wills and the like. I'm not an experienced litigator. I shall welcome your advice."

Jim said, "I'm not an experienced litigator either."

"But you had years of experience as a judge. Would you like to hear my strategy, such as it is?"

For the next hour, the three of them discussed the law of negligence and wrongful death. Alec was sharp. Inexperienced, yes, but a quick study. Jim was reassured. Between the two of them, Ernie would be well represented. Some judges on the court would bristle at a young lawyer's inevitable gaffs, but some would give him plenty of leeway, feeling sympathetic towards an eager-to-learn novice.

Midway through the hour, Alec cracked the window to let some air into his office. It reminded Jim of his early days in the law. Tiny office, bad air. Creature comforts meant nothing to Jim in those days. He had wanted to be the best lawyer he could. Times had changed; boundaries had fallen and opportunity beckoned, at least in theory, but his sense was that paths forward for the young were less clear than in his youth. Somehow it had been easier when civil rights and Vietnam had animated people, when the Cold War defined good guys and bad guys. He wondered if he was just chanting an old man's mantra – 'things were better in my day, sonny' – but he *wasn't* saying things had been better: better-defined paths, clearer choices, that's what he was saying.

He realized Alec had finished outlining his strategy and was waiting for his verdict. "I like your thinking: Degregorio is Goliath, Ernie is David. Most juries will be sympathetic to that."

Alec brightened. "I was nervous about what you'd say."

"But don't overdo it, or it'll sound like whining. Degregorio lost his son and you have to be sympathetic to that, if not to the remedy he seeks."

Outside Alec's office, Jim and Ernie stood talking. "So you think he'll do okay?" Ernie asked.

"Yes. And if he falters, I'll be there to catch him."

Jim took the #69 bus home and gingerly let himself in his house. He wandered through the living room and into the kitchen without turning on the light. Something was bothering him. Had he half-expected another threatening note? He sat at the table trying to read his mind until the dark became oppressive.

When the reason for his nerves came to him: how bereft he felt now that the portrait of Joyce was the emotional equivalent of a daguerreotype.

He climbed the stairs to the third floor and sat at his desk. After staring through the partially closed blinds, gathering his thoughts, he turned on his desk lamp and put pen to paper.

Dear Joyce,

This is a goodbye letter. I have kept you alive in my heart and mind, but for my own well-being, I must let you go. Don't get me wrong. I still love you and always will, but you are not coming back and I am moving on whether I choose to or not, so I choose to as of now.

You set the standard for me. It will be very hard for any other woman to measure up or come close, but even a minor love would be welcome at my age. I hope you understand. You were a wonderful wife, a wonderful companion, and didn't we have a good time? I loved every minute. Well, almost every minute. You understand.

I don't think there is a template for marriage. I think each marriage makes its own template, and I wouldn't suggest ours would work for others. The two of us have to rank high on the world's list of most opinionated people. Neither of us gave an inch when we thought we were right, which was always. But we loved each other throughout our standoffs and squabbles. I think it's pure crap that spouses have to take turns giving in for a marriage to succeed. Hold your ground but de-escalate battles before they damage the marrow – Judge Randall's Rx for a long marriage. Pay the cashier on the way out.

I do wish we had had children. Actually, I wish that now more than when you were alive. A daughter, I'd love to have a daughter. She wouldn't replace you but we'd know each other so well we could talk candidly about most things; not everything, but most. That would be nice.

I have met a woman. Harriet Malcolm. She is interesting and nice, and I can find no fault with her, but we aren't going to jell as a couple. I'm not sure I'll even see her again. If I do, it will be with low expectations for a lasting relationship. I don't know why I'm telling you this. It's none of your business. You are a portrait on the mantel, and I don't answer to portraits.

Goodnight, dear Joyce. The next time I write or talk to you, it will be with acknowledgment that you are gone and I am talking to myself. That sucks, it truly does. But it's time. I'm rambling. Guess I'm reluctant to say goodnight.

Love,

Jim

He sat still for a moment, then reread the letter. Satisfied, he carried it downstairs to the mantlepiece, folded it neatly in thirds, and slid it beneath Joyce's portrait.

10

At certain times of day the light over the Connecticut River valley was haunting. Like now, late evening. Light is to earth as a potter's hands are to clay. This evening the valley looked shallow, the river near. The ridges he loved so much seemed leveled as by a trowel. In a minute the light would change and the scene would be transformed. Light, time, hold still at the optimal moment please, the director shouts, but the lighting crew doesn't listen.

This was his first visit to the Vermont house since Joyce's portrait had become a relic, and his loneliness felt newly minted. Perhaps it's fortunate time doesn't stand still, or we'd never move on – perhaps stage-hands know more than directors – but time can hurt as well as heal.

How long had he been sitting there? Dusk had given the river valley cover to duck and run, and it was nowhere to be seen.

He stood, stretched, walked to the kitchen and looked to see what he had in the fridge. Only frozen lasagna left over from last visit. Lasagna it was, good it wasn't.

He slept well despite a bad dinner, waking only once to go to the bathroom. Near dawn, loud banging startled him. For frightened moments he lay in the dark, remembering the threatening note. As his mind cleared, he identified the sounds as howling wind followed by banging. He looked out the bedroom window. Trees were bending and shaking, their branches slamming the wall. Wind, nothing more sinister than wind. Go back to sleep.

In the morning he sat down to review the court filings in the civil suit of Degregorio v. Farrell. Anger coursed through every word of the dry documents – Jim wondered whether Degregorio was vengeful by nature or whether losing a son had sent him over the edge. Vengeance or grief, Degregorio had a decent chance of winning. Inexperienced Alec Mixner had to hit a home run his first time at bat in order for Ernie to win, which meant a lot was riding on Jim's help.

Jim drove back to Cambridge a day later. His first order of business was a meeting at The Long Gone with Ernie and Alec. The early morning crowd had fueled up and gone, replaced by the all-day hardcore.

"I spent the past two days in the peace and quiet of Vermont reviewing the court filings, and I think we stand a chance. I can't promise anything, of course, but judges can spot a vindictive man a mile away, and Vincent Degregorio is a vindictive man."

Alec said, "While you were away, I got a call from a reporter asking about Ernie's juvenile record."

"What did you tell him?"

"That Ernie's record had been wiped clean when he turned eighteen and has no bearing on this suit."

"Good for you. That shows the lengths Degregorio will go to win. The reporter didn't learn about Ernie's juvenile record on his own. Degregorio or his lawyers must have told him. Let's talk strategy. Standard procedure in civil cases where damages are being sought is for the case to be settled before it goes to trial. After Degregorio's lawyers scare the crap out of you – or try to – they may well offer a settlement. Some sort of public shaming of Ernie in exchange for token damages. If a settlement is not offered or if you choose not to accept one and the case goes to trial, we can expect Degregorio's lawyers to milk the pathos for all it's worth. Witness after witness will testify to what a fine young man Vincent, Jr., was, how full of potential, and what a tragic shame that such a promising life was cut short by the callousness and negligence of one Ernie Farrell. And let me be blunt: if I had put you on the stand in the criminal trial, you would have lost because your attitude at the time was sullen and contemptuous. You have matured since then, for which I give you credit, but make no mistake – a bad attitude can lose this case for you. It will play right into Degregorio's hands. Understood?"

Ernie answered without hesitation. "Understood."

"Good. A lot depends on it. Now what do you two think about a settlement, if one is offered?"

"I won't admit guilt," Ernie said. "I can't."

"Think carefully. Weigh the alternatives. If I'm correct, they might accept an admission of simple negligence, not gross negligence, and the statement could be worded to make your driving sound like the kind of carelessness we all are guilty of sometimes. Think about it."

They talked for another half hour, then Jim walked home. On the way he passed the hospital where Joyce died. For the first time he could remember, her death seemed distant. Degregorio will do anything to win, Jim thought to himself. How much of Degregorio's drive was the need to vindicate his son's death, and how much an inherent need to win?

Jim's mood hovered at slow burn for the next few days. This too would pass, he knew, but he was tired of crappy moods, so he called Harriet Malcolm even though he knew their fledgling relationship would collapse if he leaned on her for support. "I'd like to see you again."

"Jim, you're a nice man, but I think you have work to do before you can relax with a woman."

"Maybe I have to learn by doing. Will you be tense with me?"

She reluctantly smiled. "Okay, you win."

They met at a new restaurant in Kendall Square, a.k.a. Silicon Valley East. The restaurant was one of many opened to satisfy the hunger pangs of the Square's hi-tech, bio-med work force, none of whom seemed older than eighteen. Harriet chose it.

"How did you know about this place?" Jim asked when they were seated.

"A date brought me here. I liked it but I didn't like him."

The restaurant had steel beams and tall windows facing a street of construction sites and newly built labs. Jim's awkwardness from their last meeting hadn't worn off in spite of his need for a morale boost. Why had he inflicted himself on Harriet again? Harriet was talking about her school; he was barely listening. I'm being rude as hell, he told himself.

As their plates were being cleared, she said, "You're not enjoying this, are you?" There was no hostility in her voice.

"I'm sorry. My mind's on an upcoming trial."

"Shall we call it a night?"

"No, let's get dessert."

"You don't have to pretend."

"I'm not pretending. You helped me move on from Joyce's death, and I'm grateful. The least I can do is offer dessert." He hoped she found that wry.

How does an insular man who spent decades on the bench passing judgement on others lower his guard enough to let others judge him?

In the end, they both passed on dessert, settling for coffee instead. He walked her to the Red Line after dinner. Jim abandoned pretenses as they walked. "I'm sorry, sincerely sorry for the miserable evening. If I had known this would happen, I wouldn't have subjected you to it."

"Okay, get it out of your system. Apologize, apologize, apologize. Then join the living."

"You've obviously run out of patience. I don't blame you."

She didn't break stride. "You may be over Joyce, and if I helped you with that, you're welcome, but you may be too far gone for any woman. I have half a mind you want an excuse to live without women."

"Not true. I like women."

"From afar."

"What do you mean? Joyce and I were close."

"Really? It sounds to me like you two established your distances early in the marriage and that's what kept you together. Nothing wrong with that. It worked for you. I'm just saying don't involve another woman in your life until you figure out how close you want to be."

They reached the subway station.

"Can I see you again after I do?" he asked.

"Ask me then. Goodnight, Jim."

A few minutes later he found himself at his front door, having no recollection of getting home. As he fumbled for his key, cliches ran through his head to crowd out his chagrin. Home is where the heart is. Home is where when you have to go there, they have to take you in. Home is where a death threat awaits under your door. No, home is where your key will unlock the door.

11

An email from Pat Knowles, his former colleague on the bench and the judge who heard Ernie's criminal case. "I need your advice as a friend. Lunch this week?"

They arranged to meet Wednesday at a pizza parlor near the courthouse. "How are you, Jim?" she asked as she sat down. Even off the bench, her demeanor demanded respect.

"Doing well. How's work?"

"That's what I want to talk about, or rather, what it's like to be done with it."

"Meaning?"

"Retirement." She pulled her chair closer to the table. "Do you like it?"

"Are you thinking of retiring?"

"Avocado salad, dressing on the side," she said over her shoulder to the hovering waiter. "Yes," she said to Jim.

"You're not sixty-five."

"Almost. That's not the issue. I'm burnt out. The trials are blending together in my mind. I get impatient on the bench."

"Think twice before you leave."

"You left."

"It's possible to get burnt out in retirement too, you know. It's been a little over a year for me and I'm rattling around, wondering what to do."

She grew thoughtful. "When we used to have lunch together, we mainly talked about losing our spouses, we never talked about retirement. You only talked about wanting a change. Why *did* you leave the bench?"

"It's hard to know why one does things, but at the time I was fed up with the sick, cruel things people do to each other. The laying blame on others for one's own failures. I was in danger of losing my passion for justice. I wanted to hold everyone who appeared before me in contempt of court."

Pat seemed startled.

"You're surprised?"

"By the depth of your bile, absolutely."

"Come on, Pat. We know each other well."

Her avocado salad and his tuna on wheat arrived and went unnoticed.

"I thought you were just tired."

"That too."

"And that you hadn't fully recovered from Joyce's death. I thought that played a role in your decision."

Jim nodded. "See? You do know me."

"You loved her, didn't you? I remember our heart-to-hearts when she died."

"I loved her as deeply as you loved Ralph."

"But I recovered faster than you."

"I don't lower my guard easily and I don't let go easily."

She regarded him closely. "Let me guess. You recently let go."

"Good guess."

"And you're regretting retirement more than before, is that what you're saying?"

"Not necessarily. I'd probably retire again, but be warned there are downsides to it. Loneliness, for one."

"Have you tried to meet anyone, Jim?"

"Only recently, and I'm not very good at it. How about you?"

"Unlike you I have tried, but sixty-something female judges lack automatic allure."

Pat tickled him. Jim brightened. "I have an idea."

"Uh-oh, a look of mischief has entered your eyes, which spells trouble. I shudder to ask, what's your idea?"

"If you retire, we can hang out together. Watch old movies, dust off the bowling shoes, hold a gavel banging competition when things get slow."

"Like retired judges everywhere."

"You bet. We are not the stiffs litigants think we are." Jim extended his hand. "Deal?"

She reached across the table. "Deal."

A chill was in the air as Jim walked home, and midway through the long walk he gave half a thought to catching a bus. He checked to see if one was coming, but buses were infrequent because this was the good ol' USA which doesn't believe in public spending: buying a bigger TV for your man cave is good, upgrading roads, bridges and public transit is a waste of tax payer dollars. Lunch with Pat had been eye-opening. She got the joke. Good intentions notwithstanding, life is a pratfall into a sinkhole. If fools don't get you, fate will. Keep a giggle handy under your judicial robe along with your Kleenex and antacid.

Objection: he had never heard Pat giggle. Witty, often; silly, never. The record will be corrected.

His porch light was dim and he had a hard time differentiating between his keys. Have to get a brighter bulb, he told himself. The light in the pizza parlor had made Pat's skin look pallid, he realized. Noticing her skin was the first time he had allowed himself to think of her as a woman, he realized with a shock. They had both been so damn professional on the bench.

In the dim light, he fumbled for his keys.

*

He was heating soup for dinner that evening when the doorbell rang. To go with the soup, he had bought a loaf of sourdough bread on his walk home. A glass of Corbières was awaiting him at his table and he was looking forward to a quiet dinner.

He hated answering the door in the evening. Nine times out of ten it was someone soliciting money for a worthy cause: Disturb The Peace, he called all such groups. He switched on the porch light and peered through the slats – a youngish man with a beard, holding a clipboard. Jim groaned – they *always* had a clipboard.

He opened the door with what he hoped was a scowl. "Yes?"

"Good evening, neighbor."

"Who are you?"

"Soliciting signatures, sir." The young man held out the clipboard. At the top of the petition in big letters: Punish The Guilty, Free The Innocent.

Jim heard the young man saying, "There are too many of the righteous in jail, too many sinners on the streets. Don't you agree, sir?" On closer inspection, the young man wasn't so young, late thirties maybe. Behind the beard, it was hard to tell.

Jim glanced up and down the street. "Are you alone?"

"Yes, sir."

"Who sent you? Vincent Degregorio?"

The man seemed flustered. "No, sir. God sent me."

"I never sign petitions, even those endorsed by God. Good night, sir."

Jim started to close the door, but the man blocked it with the clipboard. "Sir, I am on the side of righteousness."

"No, you are outside my front door, disturbing my dinner. Goodnight."

The man backed off, and Jim slammed the door.

Jim checked to see if he had gone, then called Ted Conover, apologizing for disturbing him at home. "Ever hear of an organization called Punish The Guilty, Free The Innocent?"

"Never heard of it."

"He has really gotten to me."

"Who?"

"Vincent Degregorio. Sorry to disturb your evening."

"Did he issue another threat?"

"No. My imagination is out of control."

Conover paused. "We've known each other a long time, Jim. Forgive me for saying this, but while you were defending Ernie Farrell in court, you seemed your old self again. You are not yourself in retirement. Find a job, find a woman, volunteer your time to a homeless shelter. If you were still on the bench, you could hold me in contempt for saying that."

"If I were still on the bench, you wouldn't have needed to say that."

"So you agree with me?"

"Don't push your luck."

Ted made sense. But for the reasons he had told Natalie, he wasn't going to volunteer and he was not about to look for a job at his age. Women were out for the time being since Harriet Malcolm was the only woman he knew and he had blown his chance with her. On second thought, there was another woman, a woman he had never thought of as a woman. Without giving himself time to weigh the pros and cons, Jim called Pat Knowles and invited her to Vermont for a collegial weekend. "The house has two bedrooms. We won't even have to talk to each other, let alone get chummy. Consider it practice for hanging out together when we're both retired."

Pat laughed. "I'd be honored to see the house I've heard so much about, and I promise not to speak unless spoken to."

"Good. I'll drive."

"Do you drive like you judged?"

"What does that mean?"

Did he detect amusement in her reply? "What time will you pick me up?"

Pat looked country-ready when he arrived. To see her in jeans was a jolt. The public would be shocked to see the clothes some judges wear beneath their robes, but Jim had never seen Pat in jeans. When she climbed in the front seat beside Jim, Pat looked as formidable as she did on the bench. Until he saw her eyes – which soaked in the scenery, which looked ready for anything. The eyes of a person hungry for new experiences, eager for amusement.

"Can you cook?" she asked.

"Not at all."

"Me either. Are there restaurants near you?"

"No, I'm so far north there are no restaurants. Of course there are restaurants! Where do you think I live? Baffin Island?"

"You're very touchy off the bench."

"I'm already sorry I invited you."

"A year's probation for that remark."

"You can't sentence me. I have ex-judge immunity."

The drive seemed shorter than when he drove alone. Neither he nor Pat said much, but he felt very comfortable with her in the car. When they reached the street that climbed to his house, he slowed. The street was narrow and coursed along just below the top of the ridge. He hadn't realized how small his house was until he saw it through Pat's eyes. How had he and Joyce fit into it without squabbling? The answer was they hadn't. Two opinionated people, they bickered, argued, and fought; Joyce the vocal one, Jim the stubborn one. But the fights were confined by unspoken rules and never degenerated into name calling. In a way, the squabbles had been the glue that held them together.

"It looks cozy."

"Cramped, is more like it."

He fumbled with his keys, trying the key to the Cambridge house first, corrected his mistake and opened the door.

The house smelled of trapped air. He never knew what caused the characteristic smell – mouse droppings mixed with dust mixed with stray propane fumes? – but the smell was lying in wait, ready to leap up at his face like a happy puppy whenever he entered.

"Here we are." He switched on the light.

"Jim, it's charming."

He suddenly thought so too, even though charm was not an attribute that usually registered with him. "You're right, it is."

Pat stood in the middle of the floor. "The proportions are perfect. The view spectacular. I feel right at home."

"Let me show you to your bedroom." He led her down the short hall. His bedroom overlooked the valley, hers the ridge. He switched on her light. "I hope it's okay."

She stepped in. "Okay? It's ideal."

"Settle in, then we'll toast hanging out."

He opened the shades in his bedroom and went back to the living room, making a mental note to get a brighter bulb for the second bedroom. Pat emerged some minutes later and immediately went to the window overlooking the valley.

"You must spend all your time in this room," she said.

"Pretty much so. I eat here, read here. This room is the house, as far as I'm concerned."

"It couldn't be nicer." She stood for another moment, then turned to him. "What about our toast?"

She drank whiskey neat; he stuck to wine. He handed her glass to her. "What shall we toast?"

"I thought we were toasting hanging out."

"You're right. Here's to a weekend of hanging out."

They took a walk in the afternoon, then drove down to the village to pick up milk and bread. On the way home they made a reservation for dinner at a pricey inn further up the valley. So far the weekend had been companionable. Two friends, gender insignificant. Much more comfortable than expected or feared. Once or twice he flashed on Joyce when he saw Pat, and when that happened, he resented Joyce, which troubled him. Resent Joyce, his Joyce? Besides, any linking of the two was unfair to both. Pat wasn't auditioning to take Joyce's place, she was just there for the weekend.

At dinner in the inn, Pat seemed to read his mind. "Is it awkward to see me in the country sanctuary you shared with Joyce?"

"I've been thinking about that very subject."

"I thought so. Well?"

"The answer is yes, and part of the awkwardness is how natural it feels once I get past the initial jolt of 'who is this woman and what is she doing here?'"

The drinks came, and Jim offered a toast. "To our years together on the bench. To our friendship. To hanging out."

She clicked his glass.

"I like the inn," she said a moment later. "How is the food?"

"Not bad. I'm a picky eater, and they manage to please me."

Pat gave him a look of mock horror, eyebrows through the roof. "You're a picky eater? Easygoing Jim Randall? I don't believe it."

Jim narrowed his eyes. "Don't start, madam. You're off the bench. No gavel or robe to protect you."

Jim had fish, Pat had lamb. "How is yours?" he asked.

"Scrumptious."

"Can I get something off my chest before I have more to drink? If I don't it's going to bother me all weekend."

Pat stopped chewing. She looked worried. "What is it?"

"Vincent Degregorio has gotten to me."

"You told me about the note left under your door. Has there been something else?"

"A harmless religious nut came to my door the other night asking me to sign a petition, and I almost called the police. I see Degregorio's hand in everything. In my years on the bench, I never got this rattled."

"Have you made other enemies besides Degregorio? On the bench or off?"

"Not that I'm aware of. I put a lot of people behind bars and surely some of them hold a grudge, but I'm not aware of anyone besides Degregorio out to get me."

"I've received my share of threats while I've been on the bench," Pat said, "but they've been amateurish. Angry defendants yelling at me as they're led out of the courtroom, that sort of thing."

"I got those too, but this feels different. Maybe because Degregorio has demonstrated a self-serving concept of which laws apply to him and which don't, and he has the money to hire people to do his dirty work."

"My advice is stay alert but don't drive yourself crazy by constantly looking over your shoulder."

"Good advice. Thank you. Now we party."

Pat smiled. "That's what I came for."

They lingered over wine and had too much to drink. "Way past my bedtime," Jim said when they finally returned to the house, "but this is a special occasion. How about a nightcap?"

"Drunkard."

In the living room, he settled into his chair with his wine, Pat adjacent to him on the sofa. "This is nice," she said. "Who knew you could be such fun?"

Jim scowled. "Don't you dare call me fun."

Pat chuckled. "Fun, fun, fun."

"Speaking of which, have you made up your mind about retirement?"

"Speaking of which?"

"Do not try to follow my logic, it is sui generis."

"Sui tipsy, I would say. No, I have not decided whether to retire."

"At least this weekend proves we can successfully hang out together. That should make your decision easier."

"Any two people can hang out together if they're drunk."

"Speak for yourself. Have you seen me take a breathalyzer test?"

"No, I have not."

"Then how do you know I am drunk?"

"You win. We hang out well together. We were born to hang out."

Time slowed in a pleasurable way. Jim felt something fateful was about to happen, and that he was supposed to know what came next. Then he knew. Self-awareness in the nick of time. "Permission to hug the judge, Your Honor."

"Only if you will shut up."

He crossed to the sofa and settled in, surprised by the depth of his cushions. "I'm about to put my arm around you. You tell me if it makes you uncomfortable."

"I'm poised to object." She straightened up.

When his arm was around her, he checked. "Okay, so far?"

"For God's sake, Jim, be quiet."

The feel of a woman other than Joyce in his arms was so startling, Jim almost cried out. But once that passed, Pat felt familiar. Were women interchangeable? Did Pat equal Joyce, and Joyce equal Pat? Pat noticed his reaction and asked what was wrong.

"Nothing's wrong. What startles me is how normal it feels to have my arm around you. What does that say about my feelings towards Joyce?"

"That is the most romantic thing I've ever heard."

"I'm sorry. I'll shut up. Where were we?"

"Calling it a night. No offense, Jim, but I'm not interested in being your bridge to the future. Get over the past, then we'll see."

"I thought I had. Then please consider this a collegial kiss, nothing more." He kissed her with as much dignity as possible. They both chuckled when it was over.

"All passion spent," she murmured.

"I have a rule. I don't get serious about any woman who quotes Milton after I kiss her."

"You have a rule about that?"

"Yes, from my vast experience with women who quote Milton."

They didn't tarry on the sofa. They went to their separate rooms, two dazed boxers going to their corners between rounds. He lay in bed feeling stupid and guilty in equal measure. Who in their right mind would mention a late wife when he had another woman in his arms? And why did he feel a lingering loyalty even after his rethink of his marriage? Joyce was gone and no amount of homage to her memory could bring her back – continued fealty hurt him, didn't help her. Yet loyalty has inherent value, he had always believed and still did – loyalty was not spare change to be tossed into a tip jar.

In the darkness, it came to him: No need to distance himself from Joyce's memory, or reject the inherent value of loyalty, just move on. Honor her memory and move on.

Indirection and darkness, thinking's best friends.

In the morning before Pat awoke, Jim drove to the village to buy the Sunday papers. She was up when he returned to the house. "Did you sleep well?" he asked.

"Like a log. You?"

"Same here." He held up the thick newspapers triumphantly. "Digital future be dammed!"

They ate breakfast in the living room overlooking the valley. The morning light show was underway. "I drank more than I should last night. Did I embarrass either of us?" he asked.

"I couldn't tell. I exceeded my limit, too."

"You were more cogent than I," he said.

"Did you apologize to Joyce when you were alone?"

"I wouldn't call it an apology. Did you to Ralph?"

"No. I settled debts with Ralph's memory long ago. Do you regret our kiss?"

Jim didn't hesitate. "No, I loved it."

"Good. You're making progress."

"Where do you and I go from here?"

"Home. I go back to work tomorrow."

"You know what I mean."

"The answer is, I don't know. I don't have a master plan."

He nodded. "Me neither. I now know I enjoy your company away from the courthouse very much, and that's a start."

They drove home in late afternoon. Traffic was light. As they crossed the border into Massachusetts, Pat said, "I'm returning to court to a case of child abuse that breaks my heart. Do your hard cases come back to haunt you?"

"Very much so. Retirement does not give one immunity. Quite the opposite."

Traffic picked up as they neared Boston. Jim drove carefully in the city, automatically adjusting his driving habits to defensive when he reached Beacon Hill, where all the streets are one way and none are going the way you want. He pulled to the curb when he reached Pat's row house near the crest of the hill. "The weekend was wonderful, Pat," he said.

She slid out. "For me too. Whatever you do, don't feel guilty. Joyce and Ralph are sharing a good laugh at our expense right now."

12

He checked in with Ernie Farrell after he got home. "How is Alec coping?" he asked over the phone.

"He's in over his head. Degregorio's lawyers are piling on."

"Be specific."

"Demanding document after document. Alec is going to ask the judge to set a time limit so discovery doesn't drag on forever."

"Why didn't Alec ask me for help? That's my territory."

"I don't know."

"Let's you and I meet and talk about strategy."

"With Alec?"

"No, we need to talk about Alec."

The Long Gone was hopping when they met. In addition to the usual laptoppers, a man in a suit and tie read *The Financial Times*, a double first for The Long Gone.

Jim started. "I'll sit down with Alec after this, but I want you to understand what Degregorio is doing. It is standard procedure in civil cases to use the discovery process to intimidate the other side into reaching a settlement. Very few civil cases go to trial. Most are settled. That's why I told you to be prepared for an offer." He paused. "Okay so far?"

"Yes."

"Degregorio's lawyers are taking advantage of Alec's inexperience. Do your best to bolster his confidence. What's wrong? Why do you look as if you want to give up?"

Ernie took a painfully long time to answer. "My fault. I let down my guard after I won the first trial. I should have known better. Now I'm like, oh fuck, I have to go through this again?"

The man at the nearby table lowered his *Financial Times*. For a moment Jim thought he was going to complain, but all he did was clear his throat and resume reading.

"Yes, you do."

Ernie's shoulders slumped. "Maybe I should get it over with."

"It's too soon. If we settle prematurely, Degregorio will dictate the terms."

Ernie nodded.

"Let me talk to Alec. He has to challenge Degregorio's lawyers every step of the way, not give an inch. And you have to be strong."

The *Financial Times* reader harrumphed and folded his paper. He stood, stuck the newspaper in his suit pocket, and strode out of the coffee shop. "Probably Degregorio's spy," Jim said.

Jim paid Alec Mixner a visit that afternoon. Jim remembered Mixner's office as tiny, but it was even tinier than he remembered.

"Judge, I'm getting clobbered with requests for police records, medical records, insurance documents, court claims, traffic tickets. I can't keep up."

"Degregorio's lawyers are bullying you. I'll show you how to frame a request for a court order limiting discovery to items directly pertinent to the case."

Alec exhaled. "I'm in over my head, Judge, I never should've taken the case."

"Don't say that. You're learning as you go. And I'm here to help in any way except sit at the defense table. You knew Ernie in high school. What was he like then?"

"Nice kid. Quiet. Kept to himself. I got to know him through the chess club. He was the best chess player by far."

"Did he talk about his father?"

"Only once. We went drinking. Ernie grew sullen, then picked a fight. I had to intervene."

"Did he fight often?"

"No, that was unusual. He had a mouth on him, but he didn't fight. He seemed to me a gentle guy who hadn't been treated gently. Bullies were his flash point. He went berserk around bullies."

"Did you two stay in touch after high school?"

"No, I hadn't heard from him until he asked me to represent him. I told him I handle real estate, not wrongful death suits. Then he told me about you, and I figured I could do the job if you gave me advice. So I accepted."

"I'm glad you did. Back the bully off. Don't let him intimidate you."

"Okay if I kick his teeth in?"

"Tell me when and where, and I'll help you."

Jim started home on foot but luck was on his side in the form of a #69 bus, which pulled to the curb just as he looked to see if one was coming.

*

Jim waited until the middle of the week to call Pat Knowles. He wanted to call sooner but didn't want to look needy.

"It's Jim Randall, your hang-out partner."

"How are you, Jim?"

"Racked with guilt."

"You're not serious?"

"Correct, I'm not. I've been remembering our weekend with pleasure."

"Me too."

"And wondering when I could see you again."

"I'm free for dinner on Saturday."

"Dinner Saturday sounds perfect."

A new restaurant had opened on Charles Street that was supposed to be good. Neutral territory. "It's near your house, so you can flee if I regress."

"Sounds ideal," she replied.

Pat was originally from Pennsylvania, had gone to Yale Law School after Smith College, but Jim knew next to nothing about her family background. So before Saturday evening, he Googled her to see what he could learn. Her father had been an executive with U.S. Steel, her mother had stayed home to raise Pat and her five siblings. After law school, Pat became a partner in one of Boston's discreet blue blood firms, a firm that the wealthy and well-connected turned to for legal advice. She had practiced there for eighteen years and served on the bench for twenty-one. Her name had been floated from time to time as a candidate for the Court of Appeals.

Armed with the information, he took the Red Line and climbed the hill to her apartment. She met him at the door. "Ready?" she asked.

"You look radiant."

"Thank you. You look calm and composed."

"Looks deceive."

The short walk down the hill to Charles Street gave him time to breathe. The restaurant was nice, although the food didn't live up to the prices. Pat was a pleasure, but Jim felt a mild letdown. The weekend in Vermont had been so eye opening he half-expected the next time to be a wow. It was pleasant and companionable; no shop talk, no hint of romance. But no wow. Pleasant, what a damning word. He wondered how she felt. They skipped desert.

He walked her home. He assumed they would say goodnight at her door. Instead, she asked, "Would you like to come in for a minute?"

Maybe she had enjoyed the evening more than he thought. "Sure."

They settled into the living room, Jim's nerves jangling. The bay windows of her living room looked out on red brick and slices of sky.

"Your living room is very you," he said, removing his coat. "Impeccable taste."

"Unplanned is more like it. I have some good cognac in the kitchen, would you care for some?"

"Wonderful."

He sat on the sofa in the bay window, his back to the street. Unconnected thoughts raced through his head. She returned quicker than he expected, handed him one of the glasses, and sat beside him. "You were Jim Randall in Vermont, you are Judge Randall tonight. Have I fallen out of favor?" She clicked glasses. "Cheers."

"Not at all. I was thinking the same about you." He sipped. "Wonderful stuff. Where did you get this?"

"It was a gift. From an admirer."

"Have there been many?"

"Very few. Dinner companions for the most part. Ralph and I had a good marriage. He was a cardiologist. His passions were Renaissance tapestries and martial arts. Our marriage made no sense, but it worked."

"He sounds like someone I wouldn't like at first."

"I didn't either. You had to get to know him before you liked him."

He put his arm around her. "This is where we left off, if I remember."

"We did."

He kissed her. "That was not a collegial kiss."

"I could tell."

He kissed her again.

"No quotes from Milton tonight," Pat said.

"But we should take it slow. I want you to be convinced I'm over Joyce. It's better if I go."

"You're not going to finish your cognac?"

"I don't want to fall in love with you, Pat. I'll finish my cognac, then go. How's that?"

"Say that again."

"I'll finish my cognac, then go."

"No, before that."

"I said I don't want to fall in love with you."

"That's what I thought you said. Are you falling in love with me?"

"I'm saying I don't want to."

"That is the second most romantic thing I've ever heard, both said by you."

"I'm not very good at this."

"We're both out of practice."

"So I don't have to worry about falling in love, you're saying."

"Oh, no. Worry like hell. I crave romance, I hunger for it."

"Now I can't tell if you're joking."

"That's for you to decide, but I agree we'll last longer if we take it slow."

"Do you?"

"Yes, now that I hear you say it."

"Why do you listen to me?"

"Jim, sweet Jim."

They kissed at the door. "I think we'll be okay from now on," he said.

"Don't be afraid," she counseled.

He hated to feel as good as he did without knowing what was ahead. Certainty is what he had sought on the bench and in life. Now all was in flux.

A package wrapped in brown paper and tied with string awaited him at home. He hadn't expected anything in the mail. The return address said Valley Books, Oxford, Mississippi.

He badly had to pee, so he put the package on the kitchen table and went into the bathroom, wondering what it could be. A book he had forgotten he ordered?

He washed his hands and fished a pair of scissors out of the kitchen drawer to cut the string. It occurred to him that maybe he should be careful, but the previous time he received a package from an unknown source, it turned out to be a pair of shoes. He would be a laughingstock if he made the same mistake again.

He cut the string and removed the wrapping paper, when it occurred to him that these days stores do not use wrapping paper and string, they use sturdy boxes and shipping tape. He hesitated, wondering. Don't be a wuss, he told himself. He unfolded the carton flaps. Inside was crumpled newspaper, and inside that, a shoebox. He removed the box from the carton and lifted the cover.

13

A siren was wailing. He had the sensation of motion. It took him a minute to realize he was in the back of a speeding ambulance. He tried to speak, but an oxygen mask covered his mouth and nose. He was not aware of pain.

An EMT leaned close to his face. "Sir, we're taking you to MGH." His voice was kind. "Lie still. We're almost there."

Jim lifted his head enough to see out the window. How strange to see East Cambridge whiz by while he was flat on his back. He wanted to salute Beauty Shop Row, say hello to the chickens in the window of the live poultry store. How many times had he heard ambulances screaming down Cambridge Street – now he was in one. The last thing he remembered before blacking out again was his gurney hitting a snag as it was lifted from the ambulance. The EMTs wrestled it free. Gently, gently, he longed to say.

His first visitor when he awoke was Pat. "How long have you been here?" he asked.

"An hour or so. You had your courthouse ID in your wallet and the hospital was searching for your next-of-kin. You came through the surgery just fine. The doctor said you're lucky. It could have been much worse."

Jim lifted his heavily bandaged hands. "How bad?"

"Your right hand is going to be fine."

"My left hand?"

"I'm sorry, Jim. You lost half of your little finger."

Jim absorbed the news stoically. He couldn't resist a straight line: "How's my face?"

She took the bait. "No uglier than usual." Pat's eyes teared. "I feel so terrible, Jim. Who did this to you?"

"Vincent Degregorio."

"Are you sure?"

"I don't have proof but who else?"

"The surgeon was amazed you weren't killed. He guesses that the bomb was homemade. Everyone at the court sends you good wishes." Pat checked the clock. "The nurse said I can't stay long. Please don't work yourself into a rage. Let the police handle it."

"I'm not in any shape to rage. I'll settle for being alive." He squeezed her hand with his good one. "Thanks, Pat."

An infection in Jim's left hand required additional surgery. He remained in the hospital for five days. The first few he found himself drifting to sleep at unpredictable moments. He wasn't sure if that was the painkillers or the shock. Each time he awoke, he had to rearrange his thinking to fit the new norm of being minus half a finger. Pat stopped by twice, the police interrogated him, and Ted Conover reported that clues were lacking because so much of the package had been destroyed by the explosion. And Ernie Farrell stopped by to see how he was doing.

"This happened because of me," Ernie said.

"Don't blame yourself."

Ernie shook his head. "I've been incredibly selfish. I virtually begged you to help me."

"Don't beat yourself up. I volunteered."

At the end of the week, Jim was transferred to a rehab hospital two blocks from his house. Strangeness piled on strangeness: from his rehab room he could glimpse the roof of his house. He stayed at the facility for another three days learning coping mechanisms, and left confident his life would eventually achieve a new normal.

Natalie flew in from Oregon to help him adjust to being home. It was great to see her. "I told you not to come. You never listen to me."

She smiled. Big, sturdy Natalie. Natalie who instilled confidence by her presence. "If I always heeded my big brother's advice, I'd be a grouch like him. I'm going to stay until you're back on your feet."

"Who's taking care of Stu while you're away?"

"His sister. She and Stu send their best."

Jim was not the same person he had been – a week and a half in hospitals had left him with tissue paper muscles and elastic-band bones – but it was wonderful to be home. The first time he climbed the stairs to his study and eased himself into his reading chair, he fell into a deep, peaceful sleep. When he opened his eyes, Pat and Natalie were standing above him.

"Hi," Jim said.

"It's wonderful to see you home," Pat said.

"It's wonderful to be home, but my little sister loves to give orders. Can you tell her not to?"

Pat smiled. "She won't listen to me."

"That makes two of us." He closed his eyes.

"Do you want to nap?" Natalie said.

"I've napped enough."

Pat apologized. "I can't stay long. I wanted to see that you're safely home."

"I appreciate what both of you are doing, but I'll be my old self again any day now."

Pat looked at Natalie. "I'm not sure I like that."

"I agree. Docile is nice for a change."

So began sessions of physical and occupational therapy, to rebuild the muscles of his left hand and to relearn the tasks of daily life. One surprise among many: he couldn't count on his hands automatically working in tandem. It was as if missing half a finger had disrupted his coordination. The lag was just a millisecond or two, but made him realize how much he took for granted about the complex machinery of hands.

One fantasy that sustained him during boring bouts of therapy was beating the crap out of Vincent Degregorio with his mutilated hands. He imagined the confrontation in detail: "look what you did to my hands, now watch what they do to you," followed by a swift right to the temple to stun the self-satisfied Degregorio, followed by repeated blows to the nose and eyes. He could feel the satisfying snap of Degregorio's nose, the thump of him hitting the ground; Jim Randall would show no mercy. The physical therapist couldn't understand why Jim was often grinning by the end of their sessions.

When he shared his murderous thoughts with Natalie, she reminded him that he was a convalescing man in his sixties, that he wasn't in the best of shape even before the explosion, and that there were laws against assault and battery. Still, it was bliss to imagine.

As he continued his physical therapy, he realized with surprise how often he previously had relied on his left hand. In his sense of himself, his left hand had been a junior partner to the right. Now, so many simple tasks had to be rethought. He could grip little with his left hand and his right hand balked at picking up the slack. To get through a day took longer because everything had to be rethought. Gradually the new configuration became second nature, but not at first.

Jim's stubbornness didn't help. His physical therapist complained to Natalie that, "Your brother challenges everything I suggest, wants to know why he should do it, and wants proof it will work," to which Natalie could only shrug.

When Jim was able to fend for himself around the house, Natalie returned to Portland and Stu. It had been two weeks. "I can't thank you enough," Jim said.

"Remember to do your exercises."

"I will."

"No, you won't. But try."

When Natalie was gone and he was alone in the house, he forced himself to stare at his hands. Hands were such a familiar part of his body that to see half a finger missing was a shock akin to entering his study and finding his bookshelves bare. He fell into depression and treated his depression by taking long walks, which did his spirits and legs good. The turning point came when – out-of-the-blue and for no specific reason – he was able to put things in perspective. If he were a concert pianist, the loss of half a finger would be a huge deal, but a retired judge has a surplus of fingers and shouldn't be greedy.

Time for reentry.

A quick text to Ernie. "I'm ready to resume where we left off. Meet me at The Long Gone to catch up?"

God bless things that don't change. God bless The Long Gone.

The regulars didn't look up from their tablets when Jim entered, let along stare at his mutilated hand as Jim had imagined they would. Ernie was already at a table. He smiled when Jim joined him. "How are you?"

"Stronger every day."

"You're looking good."

"Bullshit, but thanks."

"Better than in the hospital, for sure. Any word on who did this to you?"

Jim pulled close to keep anyone from overhearing. "Homemade device. Hard to trace."

Ernie thought about that. "Doesn't sound like Degregorio."

"Bring me up to date on what you and Alec have been doing."

For the next half hour they talked about the lawsuit, which did Jim's spirits good. To think about the law did not require ten intact fingers.

Ernie seemed satisfied with Alec. "He is very thorough, meticulous. He'll be well prepared," Ernie concluded.

"It sounds that way to me, too."

Jim experimented with manipulating the coffee cup with his reconfigured, not-quite-coordinated digits. No problem with the right hand, and if he balanced the cup carefully he could lift it with his left hand without spilling. He beamed at Ernie. "See?" Spoken too soon; the cup slipped just enough to splash coffee onto the table. Jim steadied the cup with his right hand. "All I need is a little practice."

"Don't be embarrassed."

"I could still wield a mean gavel if I had to. I need a refill. Can I get you one?"

Ernie started to stand. "I'll do it," he said.

"No, let me," Jim said.

Jim did not hide his finger from the barista, and the barista took no note. Point made. All you needed to be accepted in The Long Gone was a self-aware, post-ironic attitude. Fingers were optional.

In front of The Long Gone when they were finished, Ernie shook Jim's hand. "Glad you're back. Thank you for everything."

Rejoining the living did wonders for Jim's spirits. He found himself planning ahead instead of thinking hour-to-hour. Spending more time in Vermont was part of the plan, doing something useful with his mind another, how to combine the two the puzzle. Pat could hold the clue. He invited her to dinner at Duck, Duck, Goose.

"I'd love to," was her response. "Are you sure you're ready?"

The prospect of taking her to his favorite restaurant made him giddy. "More than ready. I'm raring to go. I want you to see my local, my neighborhood hangout, where I'm somebody."

"Where you're somebody? You mean, being a distinguished retired judge isn't enough?"

"Hell, no. It requires being a regular at Duck, Duck, Goose."

Pat came as close as she could to a giggle. "Are you still on painkillers?"

"No. Natural high."

"Control yourself at the restaurant. Remember, we're dignified."

"You are, I used to be. I'm ex-dignified."

Bruce the young owner greeted them at the door with a flourish. "It's great to see you back, Judge. We were worried about you." He gave Jim a two-handed handshake.

"It's great to be back. This is my friend, Pat Knowles."

Bruce bowed. "Welcome. I hope you enjoy your meal. Anything you need, let me know. Follow me."

On the way, Jim waved to Chris behind the bar. "When I eat here alone, that's where I sit," he explained to Pat.

Pat looked. "I can't picture you there. Do you talk to anybody?"

"I'm offended, of course I talk. I meet women. You have no idea how many. Ask Chris, the bartender, if you don't believe me."

Pat gave him a look.

Bruce seated them at a table near the window, a well-placed table from which they could scan the whole restaurant. It reassured Jim to be in Duck, Duck, Goose again. He could feel his shoulders relax. He had something to tell Pat, but it could wait; food first, love later.

Pat's face creased with appreciation when the food arrived. "This is good," she said. "From our lunches, I never would have guessed you appreciated good food."

"I don't, as a rule. If this place weren't around the corner, I never would have tried it."

"How are you healing?"

"Very well. Back to normal, or thereabouts."

"No clues yet as to who did it?"

"None."

"Jim, I know you blame Degregorio, but I'm skeptical. He seems too calculating to do something like this."

"Don't be fooled. He's a nasty, vindictive man."

"That doesn't make him a bomber."

Bruce stopped by the table to see how everything was. "Wonderful, as usual."

"Excellent," Bruce replied. "You look good, Judge."

"I feel good."

After the dinner plates were cleared, Jim told Pat what was weighing on his mind. "I've had a lot of time to think, and I'm in no mood to deny what I've learned. I am frightened of being close to a woman other than Joyce. More than frightened. Terrified." He raised his left hand. "It feels as unsettling as this. But I'm serious about you, more serious than I believed myself capable at this stage of my life. Okay to continue? I'm not scaring you off?"

"You are not scaring me off. Continue."

Another interruption: a waiter poured more wine. Jim waited until he had left. "I loved our weekend together in Vermont. It felt normal to me, like we did it all the time. I want to spend more time with you, I want to know what you're like when no one is watching, I want to know how you handle the minor irritations of daily life, and I want you to know the same about me. I'm not an easy person to get along with, I'm set in my ways, in case you didn't notice in the years we were colleagues. If you can put up with me, then I can see this leading somewhere." He sat back, relieved to get it off his chest. "How's that?"

"Jim, this has been a highly emotional time in your life. Are you sure you'll feel the same about me after the trauma fades?"

"I think so, but who knows? That's the whole point. I've wasted a lot of time waiting for certainty before I try anything new. Waiting for certainly provides a built-in excuse to do nothing. No risk, no pain, but also no gain. Now I'm taking a chance on the riskiest thing of all, love."

He watched Pat's austere face for clues. Her expression was too firm to send loud signals but so far so good. He had half-expected laughter.

Her expression eased. She looked him in the eye. "Oh, hell, Jim, I have loved you for years. Don't look so surprised. I loved you when we were colleagues but until you retired it felt illicit to admit it. Now I am free to tell you. I love you, you stubborn oaf."

There often is a time delay between change and the recognition of change, and change can come in pairs – finger lost, love found. Change is life's Lost and Found. Jim sat still while his sputtering mind searched for the right words.

Pat to the rescue. "I hope you want dessert, because I absolutely do," she said.

"Duck, Duck, Goose has wonderful deserts."

"Good. Then let's get a menu."

Jim looked over his shoulder for a waiter. "So, we continue," he said to Pat.

"Yes."

"And see what happens."

"Jim, will you stop thinking for a moment? Yes, we see what happens. First we get desert, then we see what happens."

He caught the eye of their waiter. As he approached, Jim murmured, "Their flourless chocolate cake is not to be believed."

*

Tuesday afternoon, Jim got a call from Alec Mixner. "Welcome back. Degregorio's lawyers have moved for a change of venue. Judge Larson will hear the motion on Friday. If you can't make it, don't worry."

"I'll be there."

Judge Larson, the judge assigned to the case, was new to the court. Pragmatic, careful not to reveal his hand, was the scuttlebutt that reached Jim's ears. Jim got to court early. He doubted that Degregorio himself would attend the hearing but hoped he would. As Jim waited, the desire for revenge which had filled his nights and part of his days became muted, the fury wrapped in gauze. He didn't have time to analyze why before Degregorio walked through the courtroom doors. He stood for a minute, getting his bearings, then moved forward. Jim hadn't seen him since the criminal trial. His appearance stunned Jim; he looked frail, haggard.

Jim had planned to confront him and let him know he wasn't intimidated by the bomb, but it seemed beside the point. He almost wanted to help the guy.

As Degregorio moved up the aisle towards the front of the courtroom, he spotted Jim. His slow double-take, his mournful eyes, startled Jim. To Jim's further surprise, Degregorio entered Jim's empty row and walked towards him.

"I was sorry to hear what happened to you," Degregorio said, sounding as if he meant it. "I lost my son. That was enough. I wished you no bodily harm, certainly not what happened."

Jim's mind raced. Was it possible that the scenario Jim had written and rewritten in his head to explain the bombing was wrong? Would his thoughts of revenge have to be scrapped, or at least, redirected?

If Degregorio was lying, he was artful. Jim didn't know what to believe. "Do you have any idea who did it?" Degregorio was asking.

Jin tried to temper his words, but weeks of pent-up fury are hard to blunt. "I assumed you."

"You thought *I* did it? Why on earth would you think that?"

Jim regretted speaking his mind before he was sure of his villain, but he was in too deep to stop now. "Maybe because I remember your words, 'You haven't heard the last of this.'"

Degregorio became animated. "I was talking about a civil suit, I was talking about going back to court. My God! I'm very sorry about your hand, but I had nothing to do with it. Get a grip on yourself." Degregorio strode forward, shaking his head in disbelief.

"Harder to do than before," Jim called after him.

The hearing was brief, Judge Larson no-nonsense, and the change of venue motion denied.

Jim felt like a fool. He had humiliated himself in front of Degregorio and hurt Ernie's chances for a favorable settlement. He called Pat. "I'm going up to my house in Vermont for a few days. Could I interest you in dinner after I get back?"

"You could."

"Good. Very good."

"Be careful, Jim. You'll be all alone up there, and whoever sent the bomb may try again."

His frame of mind driving north resembled the first time he had gone to the Vermont house after Joyce died. Six months passed before he dared and when he entered, the emptiness of the house pressed on his rib cage until he had trouble breathing. He had gone to the window, gazed over the valley, and in the days that followed watched sunrise after sunrise, day after day, and little by little, hour by hour, breath returned.

That was a singular experience, never – thank god – to be repeated, but this trip had a similar aura of occurring on a cusp. Whether that was good or bad, something to look forward to or something to fear, he didn't know.

Who sent the bomb if it wasn't Degregorio? He found the thought that an unknown person was out to get him more unnerving than pinning the blame on Degregorio.

He stayed in Vermont three peaceful days and three restless nights. The morning before he drove home, Casey came by to clean the house. It was the first time Casey had seen his hand since the explosion, and she gasped when she saw it.

"I read about the bomb, but it's a shock to see what it did to you, you poor man."

"Don't worry, I'm back to my grumpy self."

"Would you mind?" She closed the gap between them and gave him a quick hug.

Embarrassed, Jim growled, "Enough. Are you going to clean the house or just stand there?"

He wished he understood his mind, understood why he felt more clear-headed on the drive home than on the drive up, even though he had resolved nothing, absolutely nothing. He pulled over at the New Hampshire liquor store rest stop. Ernie had texted him. "The Long Gone tomorrow 8 a.m.?"

The Long Gone at 8 a.m. – except for their fingers moving like daddy long legs over laptop keyboards, the denizens of The Long Gone looked barely alive.

Ernie had news. "I've decided to apply to grad school. Computer engineering. I'll keep my day job and go to night school."

"A wonderful idea."

"Going to grad school will please my dad, but I'm going to do it anyway."

"Bravo, Ernie, good for you. I'll be more than happy to write a recommendation."

"That's what I was going to ask." Ernie leaned forward, eager to talk, as if a seawall had been breached. "Level with me, Judge. Based on your experience, was I subconsciously on purpose not paying enough attention to my driving when I hit Degregorio, Jr.?"

"I'm not a shrink, Ernie. I can't answer that."

"I know in my heart that I didn't intend to hurt anybody, but maybe I wanted to hit rock bottom. Maybe I wanted to screw up so badly Dad would have to help me."

"Or maybe it was an accident. Judge Knowles threw out the case against you for lack of evidence, remember?"

"She said there was insufficient proof, not that I was blameless. I'm trying to be honest about myself for a change. I'm not the loser Dad says I am, but maybe I'm not the man I imagined myself to be. Where do I fit in? I don't just mean about the accident, I mean vis-a-vis the universe. Do you see what I'm saying? Why are you smiling?"

"If this case goes to trial, I want to lend support by sitting at the defense table with you and Alec."

*

Jim called Natalie in Portland that evening to see how Stu was doing. Not well, was the answer.

"At least he seems happy. When he stares out the window, he has a smile on his face, as if enjoying a private joke. I wonder if he realizes what's happening to him."

"How sad."

"We had many happy years together, not everyone is so lucky. I have no reason to complain." She roused herself. "Is your hand fully healed?"

"Ugly as sin, but healed."

"Doing your exercises?"

"Of course I am."

"You're not, are you?"

"Not religiously, no. Stop pestering me."

"Why don't you move out here? What's holding you there?"

"Do you remember the name Pat Knowles?"

"She was a judge, yes?"

"She still is. She's been on my mind recently. I want to get to know her better off the bench."

"I'm glad, Jim. There's a lilt in your voice that's been missing since Joyce died."

"A lilt? I do not lilt. I have never lilted. Take that back."

She ignored him. "Another reason you should consider moving here is your safety. Whoever sent the bomb may not be done."

"You are at your most annoying this evening. We've been through this already. I'm not afraid. The only reason I'd come out to the Wild West is to help you with Stu."

"I appreciate that, but there's nothing you or anyone can do at the moment. We just wait."

"Okay. Seriously, let me know. I can be there on short notice."

Natalie's voice changed timber. "My wish before Stu dies is that I can speak through the fog and reach the person I married to tell him how much I love him."

"My guess is he already knows. My guess is he has felt loved by you from the moment you two met."

"But I want to tell him one more time."

"I think your love has become part of his DNA. I think he knows." Jim waited. He heard muffled sobs. "Natalie?"

"I shouldn't cry. There are people worse off."

"Yes, there are. There are always people worse off, but that doesn't mean you don't have a right to cry."

She sniffed back tears. "I feel better."

"I'm glad. You deserve to feel better."

"Does everything have to end sadly, Jim? Can't at least love have a happy ending?"

"I don't know. I haven't experienced that."

She paused. "I'm going to be embarrassed when I get off the phone. I haven't cried like this in ages."

"Call whenever you feel like crying. I have a long-distance shoulder."

14

"All rise!"

At the defendant's table: Ernie, Alec, Jim.

At the plaintiff's table: Vincent Degregorio and his attorney, Michael Loomis.

In the jury box: four women and three men.

The courtroom was nearly empty. The civil trial had none of the pizzazz of the criminal trial, monetary damages being less sexy than incarceration. That pleased Jim. He and Alec had opted for a jury trial reasoning that a jury in a case where only monetary damages were at stake was more likely to side with a salaried young man like Ernie than with a monied, ex-felon like Vincent Degregorio.

The judge for the trial was Judge Larson, a tree-trunk of a man in his fifties. Jim knew him but not well. Judge Larson entered and took his seat. "Be seated. This is a civil trial in which monetary damages are sought to compensate for the death of the plaintiff's son. Are the attorneys ready?"

"We are, Your Honor," Loomis and Alec agreed.

"Who will speak for the plaintiff?"

Loomis rose and buttoned his jacket. "I will, Your Honor."

"Mr. Loomis, you may begin."

"May it please the court. Ladies and gentlemen of the jury. The facts in this case are straightforward. A pickup truck driven by the defendant collided with a bicycle ridden by the plaintiff's son, Vincent Degregorio, Jr., an undergraduate student at Boston University, resulting in his death."

Loomis approached the jury box. The jurors watched without expression.

Loomis stopped directly in front of the jury box. He was a man in early middle age, impeccably dressed, low-keyed. "What you as members of the jury will be called upon to decide is the degree of responsibility on the part of the defendant, Ernie Farrell. It is our contention that he did not exercise the requisite degree of care and that the victim's father deserves compensation for the loss of his son." Loomis slowly spun away from the jury box. "Nothing can bring young Degregorio back to life, nor frankly, does Mr. Degregorio need the money, but wrongs should be righted where possible and finding the defendant responsible for the death of Vincent Degregorio, Jr., will help do that. Mr. Degregorio will donate any compensation he receives as a result of this trial to charity. This is not about personal gain, this is about fairness."

When it was the defense's turn to speak, Alec rose and faced the jury. He looked like a choirboy who has forgotten to brush his hair. He stared at his notes as he spoke. His words came haltingly at first

Look at the jury, look at the jury, telegraphed Jim. Midway through his opening, Alec did. He locked eyes with the jury and spoke without 'um's' and 'ah's.' From then on, he was impressive.

"We all want justice to be done, not just in court but in life. When there is a wrong, we want to right it. When someone is to blame, we seek to punish. But sometimes there is no one to blame for a tragedy, and we are reminded of the cruelty of chance and the fragility of life. Anyone can understand the grief and anger of Vincent Degregorio. No one holds that against him. But we must be careful not to let one tragedy cause another. Ernie Farrell is a young man starting out in life. He and his wife live in a one-bedroom apartment in Somerville. I assure you, Mr. Degregorio does not live in a one bedroom apartment."

Alec had hit his stride. He spoke with earnestness and fluidity. He spoke to the jury as his peers. Jim was impressed.

"Mr. Degregorio proposes to give any damages he wins in this case to charity, which is admirable, but punishing Ernie Farrell is not charitable, nor is it the best way to remember Vincent Degregorio, Jr. Charity towards Mr. Farrell, who did not cause this tragedy but has to live with it for the rest of his life, is a better way."

Alec sat down.

After a pause, Judge Larson said, "Mr. Loomis, you may call your first witness."

*

It was clear to Jim after the first day that Degregorio's lawyer intended to call every witness who could conceivably, however tangentially, help his cause. In football the tactic would be called piling on. The officers who responded to the accident were questioned at such length that Judge Larson at one point admonished Loomis. "Mr. Loomis, you have asked the same question of this officer three different ways. Pray that you do not intend to try a fourth."

"No, Your Honor."

"Thank God. Move on."

By the end of the day, the football had only moved forward five yards, and everyone in court appeared drained.

Jim huddled with Alec and Ernie as the courtroom emptied. "Nice job."

"You think? I was scared shitless," Alec replied.

"You hit your stride quickly in your opening statement."

Ernie agreed. "I thought you did great."

"Thank you, Ernie," Alec said. "Keep in mind that the standard of proof in a civil trial is a 'preponderance of the evidence,' not 'beyond a reasonable doubt' as in the criminal trial. Degregorio has a better chance of winning this time."

"I remember."

"But I think we have a shot."

Jim was in a reflective mood that night. He fixed himself a quick supper, then sat in his study reading wrongful death cases to see if he had missed anything the first time. Courts have wide latitude in wrongful death cases, and it wasn't difficult to find a case that supported whichever stance one chose to take. The human element counted more than in cases, say, of breaking and entering. Which is why he and Alec had wanted a jury. As flawed as they could be, juries usually brought common sense to their deliberations.

At one point in his life Jim had toyed with being a teacher. He had settled on law more or less by default, a "you-can't-go-wrong-if-you-study-law" kind of choice. Then, to his surprise, he found he loved the logic of the law, even when it constituted a dodge, a feint, from the facts of a case. The law's need for logic was akin to Jim's need for routine. He recognized the value of common sense – common sense grounded the law in reality. But logic was the law's GPS.

Joyce had contended that emotions, more than logic, ruled life.

"I don't disagree," Jim replied to her more than once. "But without logic, there would be no consistency to the law. Everything would depend on the whims of the judge and jury."

"Doesn't it anyway?" she had replied.

"No, absolutely not. There's are statutes, regulations, and a body of case law behind every verdict." Jim was adamant on this point. It was what he did for a living, after all. This had been a running argument between them, but gradually he came to accept it as part of their marriage's routine.

He rose out of his chair, fed up with his refusal to let the past rest in peace. He had wanted to be a teacher, but he'd been happy in the law and happy with Joyce. Full stop. Why reassess? Did he really need to whittle the past to fit the present?

The second day of the trial was much like the first. Poor Ernie. To hear every tiny component of that fateful commute replayed, analyzed and re-analyzed, had to be agonizing for him. He had left his office to drive home on an ordinary evening, and now every second of his commute was being scrutinized.

The timing of the accident dominated the second day. The time-line of the accident was recited, minute by minute, and boldly displayed on a chart professionally prepared by Loomis. Where Degregorio had found his boatload of expert witnesses, Jim could only guess. Maybe they were all members of a family of experts. Did babies born with the surname Expert get to choose their area of expertise or were they pigeon-holed at birth?

Loomis rested the plaintiff's case on Friday.

"What do you think?" Alec asked Jim in the lobby.

"They presented a strong case for carelessness. It will be up to the jury to decide if the carelessness reached the level of negligence." Jim turned to Ernie. "Are you holding up?"

Ernie nodded grimly.

Jim gripped his arm. "You will come out of this in one piece, you won't be ruined. If the jury finds against you, I predict you will get off lightly. Trust me."

Jim went to sleep Friday night thinking of the trial, but he dreamt of being trapped in a dark tunnel. In his dream he could see a brightly lit exit sign on the only door in sight, but the door was locked. He awoke in the morning feeling as if he hadn't slept.

He thought of Pat. He marveled at how thoroughly the prospect of having dinner with her pleased him; she had meant more to him when they worked together than he realized. The relentless push of life. The pinhead-size bugs in his Vermont kitchen, which drove him to distraction in certain seasons, darted faster than the eye could see to avoid being crushed by his thumb. Why did they care? Did they not realize they were dots, of no consequence to the universe?

Alec Mixner, Ernie, and Jim met at the courthouse coffee shop early Monday morning. It was the kind of bright, clear morning that snaps one awake. Ernie's nerves were as taut as those of a pinhead bug sensing a thumb. "I know what will happen when you put me on the witness stand. I'll tense up, and the jury will think I'm arrogant."

Alec tried to calm him. "It's unlikely I'll put you on the stand today, but when I do, just follow my lead."

Alec had located two new eyewitnesses to the accident. Jim was chagrined he had found neither for the criminal trial even though it didn't affect the outcome.

The first of the two was a woman in her forties. "Where were you standing, Mrs. Pryor?" Alec asked.

"I was waiting to cross the street."

Alec went to a chalkboard on which he had mapped the street Ernie and Vincent Degregorio, Jr., had been traveling and the entrance to the Interstate. "You were standing here?" he indicated a corner across from the entrance.

"Yes."

"Did you have a clear view of what happened?"

"I could see a pickup truck turning onto I-90, and I could see a bicycle approaching from behind. I lost sight of the bicycle when it reached the pickup truck."

"Could you see the driver of the pickup?"

"Clearly."

"How would you describe his actions?"

"He looked to his right before he made his turn."

"Did he seem focused on what he was doing?"

"Objection, leading the witness," Mr. Loomis said.

"I'll allow it," Judge Larson ruled.

"I'll rephrase the question, did Mr. Farrell seem focused on his driving?"

"I would say so, yes."

"As far as you could tell, he was not distracted?"

"As far as I could tell."

"No cell phone? No texting?"

"Not that I could see."

"How about the bicycle rider? What did you observe about him?"

"He was going very fast, faster than the cars, that's why I noticed him."

"Did you observe anything else about the bicycle rider?"

"I'm so used to bicycles breaking the rules, I wasn't paying close attention. I just noticed his speed."

"Could you tell if he was looking where he was going?"

"No, I couldn't."

"Is it possible he wasn't?"

"Objection."

"Sustained."

"No further questions of this witness"

Loomis approached the witness. "Morning, Mrs. Pryor."

"Good morning," she replied.

"Had Mr. Farrell just gotten off the phone?"

"I have no way of knowing."

"Had he just been texting?"

"There again, I don't know."

"In fact he could have been distracted by the phone or a text just before he turned, isn't that correct?"

"I guess so."

"Something that distracts doesn't have to happen simultaneously with a lapse of attention, does it? It can happen before?"

"I guess that's right."

"Thank you. No further questions."

The second new witness was the owner of a dry cleaners situated across the street from the entrance.

"Where were you when the accident happened, Mr. Macintosh?"

"I had come out of the shop to help our delivery driver unload his van."

"Would you please indicate on the chalkboard where you and the van were?"

Mr. Macintosh drew a rectangle for the van and an X behind the van. He turned to face Alec.

"Your van was parked cater-corner across the street from the Interstate entrance, is that correct?"

"Yes."

"And you were standing behind the van helping the driver unload?"

"Correct."

"Did you have a clear view of the traffic turning onto the Interstate?"

"Yes, I did."

"And what did you observe?"

"A pickup truck driven by the defendant began a right turn onto the entrance ramp and hit a bicycle that was coming up rapidly from behind."

"Did you see the accident?"

"Not the moment of impact, no."

"What happened after you lost sight of the bicycle?"

"I heard a loud thumping and crushing noise, unlike anything I had ever heard."

"Were you still watching the entrance ramp?"

"No, I had stopped looking just before I heard the noise."

Alec paced in front of the witness stand. "Before you stopped looking, did you observe the driver of the pickup, the defendant Mr. Farrell?"

"I did, through the driver's side window."

"Did you have a clear view?"

"Yes."

"And what did you observe?"

"Nothing out of the ordinary. Mr. Farrell glanced to his right before he made his turn."

"He glanced to his right?"

"Yes."

"Did it seem like a cursory glance? A careless glance?"

"No, sir. It was the kind of glance that drivers make all the time to see if anyone is in the right lane."

"Thank you. Your witness."

Mr. Loomis approached on behalf of the plaintiff. "You said you had a clear view of Mr. Farrell through the driver's side window of his pickup truck. For how long did you observe him before he made his turn?"

"Only a second or two."

"Only a second or two. Not long enough to see what he had been doing just before he made the turn, is that correct?"

"Objection, leading the witness," Alec claimed.

"I'll allow it," Judge Larson said. "This is cross-examination, Mr. Mixner. Mr. Loomis has wide latitude."

"I could not see what Mr. Farrell was doing before he made his turn."

"And you only observed him for a second or two."

"Correct."

"So you have no way of knowing what he was doing a few seconds before he made his turn? Something could have distracted him just before he entered your line of sight?"

"Yes, that's possible."

"Thank you." Mr. Loomis looked knowingly at the jury. "I have nothing else for this witness, Your Honor."

By the end of the afternoon, Alec had called his own experts to the witness stand, not as many as Degregorio, but enough to be credible. Jim was impressed with Alec's questioning. For a lawyer with scant trial experience, he was deft on his feet.

He told Alec so outside the courthouse at the end of the day. "You seem comfortable in court, are you?"

Alec thought. "Not comfortable, no, but prepared. Ernie, I'll put you on the stand tomorrow. Are you ready?"

"As ready as I'll ever be."

*

Ernie on the witness stand looked diminished. Everyone looks diminished on a witness stand. Since Ernie had
not testified in the criminal trial, he had no experience as
a witness, and he did badly at first. His nerves read as contempt for the process. From the defense table Jim made
subtle hand signals to Alec to slow the questioning down.

Alec had offered to let Jim question Ernie, but Jim had
declined. "You're doing a fine job. It will confuse the jury
if I take over."

Alec paced before the witness stand. "Mr. Farrell, take
us back to the evening of the accident, and walk the jury
through what happened. What time did you leave the
office?"

Ernie shifted his weight. "About 8 p.m."

"And were you in a special hurry to get home?"

"No. It was a usual day."

Alec turned and paced in the other direction. "Describe
for the jury your state of mind as you drove home."

"Normal. The day had gone well."

"Husbands and wives sometimes fight. Did you and
your wife squabble before you left for work?"

"No, we didn't. Janet got up earlier than I did. We only
saw each other for a minute before she left for work."

Alec stopped pacing. "You texted her before you
turned."

"Yes. To tell her I was on my way home."

"Were you concentrating on your driving?"

"I was. I always do."

"Have you had many accidents?"

"No. This was the first one. I've never even gotten a ticket. Understand, please, I'm used to multitasking. That's the way my mind works."

Alec resumed pacing.

"Take us back to that moment and describe for the jury exactly what you did and what went through your mind."

Ernie turned in his seat to face the jury, as Jim had instructed him to do. "Okay, as I neared the entrance to the Interstate, I texted Janet to tell her I'd be home in a few minutes and got into the right lane. When I reached the interstate entrance, I looked to my right to see if anyone had come up beside me, then began my turn."

"Did you see anybody when you looked to your right?"

"No, I did not. I had seen a bicycle further back, but I didn't see it when I looked before I started my turn."

"When happened after you started your turn?"

Ernie faltered. He looked at his hands. "I heard a terrible sound, a sort of grinding, crunching sound like nothing I had heard before. I thought maybe I had hit a trash can on the curb or something. I didn't know. Then I saw a pedestrian frantically waving at me...." Ernie stopped to collect himself.

Alec was careful not to block the jury's view of Ernie. "Take your time. Tell us everything you remember."

Ernie slowly exhaled. "I stopped my truck and jumped out. I still didn't know what had happened. I ran around curbside and saw a bicycle beneath my wheels." Ernie's shoulders shook. "I was stunned and it took a second before I realized I was also seeing an arm under my car." Ernie buried his face in his hands and sobbed. "Forgive me," he said, his voice muffled. "Give me a second."

Judge Larson looked down from the bench and asked, "Would you like to take a recess?"

Ernie shook his head. "No, Your Honor. I'd like to continue."

Judge Larson nodded to Alec, who approached Ernie. "What happened then, Mr. Farrell? Take your time."

"I got back in my truck and called 911. I guess someone beat me to it because the dispatcher said they were already on their way."

Alec addressed the judge. "Your Honor, the defense submits the audio recording of the 911 call and requests that it be marked for exhibit."

"Mr. Loomis, do you have any objections?"

"No, Your Honor."

"The recording shall be marked as defense exhibit number thirty-four."

"Your Honor, we would like the jury to hear the recording before we proceed."

"Mr. Loomis?"

"No objections, Your Honor."

"Proceed."

The clerk punched a button and the dispassionate voice of a male dispatcher filled the courtroom. "911. What is the location of your emergency?"

Ernie's voice, rattled, young: "I need an ambulance. I hit somebody on a bike at the 30 north exit of I-93. Please hurry."

"We're on the way. ETA 3 minutes. Are you a witness to the accident?"

"I'm the driver. Oh, god, I can't believe this. My father will kill me."

Alec nodded to the clerk, who turned off the machine. The courtroom was as silent as a crypt. Alec spoke softly to Ernie. "Tell the jury what happened next."

"The next thing I know, I heard sirens and then I was in a police car. They took me to the station where I made a statement."

Alec went back to the table and held up a piece of paper. "I am holding plaintiff's exhibit number three. Is this the statement you gave at the police station?"

Ernie took a look. "Yes, that's it."

"Is that your signature on the statement?"

"Yes, it is."

Alec pointed to a paragraph in the statement. "Would you please read the third paragraph?"

Ernie took the statement and began to read. "I was aware of a bike lane to my right so I looked before I made my turn to be sure no one was coming. I had passed a bicycle rider several blocks back, but I didn't see anyone coming when I looked a second time. I texted my wife 'be home soon', then began my turn."

"Were you texting your wife while you turned?"

"No, sir. I finished my text before I turned."

"Thank you." Alec took the statement from Ernie. "The full statement will be available for the jury during their deliberations." Alec walked a few steps towards the defense table. "One final thing, Mr. Farrell. You sounded badly shaken on the 911 tape. Rattled, scared. Were you?"

"I'm still rattled. I will never get over seeing what I saw."

"Your witness." Alec returned to the defense table, and Loomis approached the witness stand. He took his time.

"Good morning, Mr. Farrell."

"Good morning."

"Are you scared of your father?"

"Objection!" Alec was on his feet.

"Sustained. Rephrase, Mr. Loomis."

"On the 911 tape you say your father will kill you. Has that affected your testimony?"

"I have told the truth."

Loomis turned to one side. "It would be human to shape the truth to fit your fear, Mr. Farrell. All of us do it. Are you sure you're not doing so now?"

Alec was on his feet again, but Ernie answered calmly, "I'm sure."

Loomis took two steps towards the jury box, stopped and turned towards the witness stand. "I don't know about you, Mr. Farrell, but at the end of a long day, I'm in a hurry to get home. Sometimes I'm impatient, cut corners. Does that describe your state of mind on the evening of the accident?"

"No. My day was no longer than usual and no more stressful."

"You drive the same route home every evening?"

"Yes."

"Do you ever think of things other than your driving when you are on the way home?"

"Of course. Everyone does."

"But most commutes don't end in death."

"You don't have to remind me."

"You testified that you are used to doing several things at once. Perhaps a one-track mind would be a good thing to have when you're driving."

"Objection!" Alec barked.

"Sustained. Questions, Mr. Loomis. Not quips."

Loomis approached the witness stand. "Remember, Mr. Farrell, you are under oath. Do you stick by your statement to the police that you were not texting when you made your turn?"

"I do."

"You're certain there wasn't even a second of overlap?"

"I am certain I had finished texting by the time I started my turn. There is no doubt in my mind. None at all."

"Was your mind still on what you had texted your wife? Were you worried your wife would be upset with you for being late?"

"She's used to my hours. I wasn't any later than usual."

"So it was a routine text?"

"Absolutely."

"Didn't linger in your mind? No second thoughts about it?"

"None. No."

"A lot depends on your word, sir. A young man is dead, and a father seeks recompense. You wouldn't shade the truth to protect yourself, would you?"

Jim couldn't help himself. He jumped to his feet for the first time during the trial. "Objection!" he called in his most judicial voice.

Judge Larson looked mildly amused. "Welcome, Judge Randall. Where have you been?"

"Sorry, Your Honor," Jim sat. "Mr. Mixner is Mr. Farrell's attorney, not me. Reflex action. I apologize."

"Actually, I agree with you. Objection sustained. Mr. Loomis' last question was more of a statement than a question. The jury will disregard it. Continue, Mr. Loomis."

"I'm almost done. One final question. Mr. Farrell, is it true that you flunked the driving test twice before you got your license?"

Ernie turned ashen. "Yes."

"You flunked twice?"

"That's correct."

"No further questions."

Jim and Alec hastily leaned their heads together. "Did you know about this?" Jim asked.

"Not a clue," Alec answered.

Judge Larson intervened. "Mr. Mixner, do you have more questions for this witness?"

Alec pushed back from the table and rose to his feet. "Yes, Your Honor." He approached Ernie. "How long have you had your driving license, Mr. Farrell?"

"Let me think. Fifteen, no sixteen years."

"In those sixteen years, how many accidents have you had?"

"None until now."

"And how many traffic tickets have you received?"

"None."

"Do you consider yourself a safe driver?"

"Yes, sir."

"But you failed the driving test twice."

"I was young and smug. I thought I didn't have to study for the written exam. I thought I could wing it. I was wrong."

"Did you pass the driving portion of the test?"

"I did. Both times."

"Thank you. No further questions."

"Mr. Loomis, rebuttal?"

"No, Your Honor."

Alec spoke firmly. "The defense rests, Your Honor."

"Very well. Given the hour, we'll adjourn until tomorrow. Closing arguments will begin at nine a.m. Ladies and gentlemen of the jury, at the conclusion of the closing arguments, I will read you your instructions, and then you will begin your deliberations. I remind you, you are not to talk about the trial to anyone including fellow jurors until you are in the jury room and have begun deliberations." He banged the gavel and whisked out of the courtroom.

Jim decompressed with a cognac after dinner. He was in his study, letting his mind sort through the day's testimony when the phone rang. It was Alec.

"Any loose ends I should consider before tomorrow?"

"I don't think so. I was just reviewing today's testimony in my mind. I'm pleased with how Ernie did once he warmed up, and you did fine."

Alec agreed about Ernie. "I thought Ernie handled himself well. A lot will depend on the jury's sympathies."

Jim said, "What I don't know and hesitate to guess is what the verdict will be. It's a close call. Could go either way."

"Any suggestions for my summation?"

"Keep doing what you're doing. Be confident, but not too confident. Respectful of the deceased, quietly miffed at Degregorio for going after the little guy. Only one small suggestion," Jim said.

Alec replied. "Let me guess. Reinforce the idea that Degregorio, Jr., could have been the reckless one. He was going very fast on his bike, according to eyewitnesses. We have no way of knowing whether he was paying attention to the traffic. Not fair to place all the blame on Ernie Farrell. It that approximately what you were thinking?"

"Yes. Get some sleep. Good luck tomorrow."

*

Judge Larson gaveled the courtroom to order the next morning. "Mr. Loomis, your closing statement please."

Loomis approached the jury. He seemed grim, a man on a mission. He stopped in front of the foreman.

"Good morning. The overarching fact in this case is that a promising young man is dead. It is our contention that the negligence of the defendant caused the death. The father of the deceased seeks recompense, not to enrich himself but to gain some semblance of peace of mind."

Loomis turned until he half-faced the jury, half-faced Ernie. "No one contends that Mr. Farrell intentionally killed Mr. Degregorio. This was a tragic accident. Some accidents are acts of God, some are acts of nature, some are acts of negligence. We contend this accident was caused by Mr. Farrell's negligence. You have heard witnesses say Mr. Farrell was looking down at his lap just before the accident. We'll never know for certain because the time of accident is based on eyewitness testimony and police estimates, but even taking Mr. Farrell at his word that he wasn't texting his wife at the exact moment of the accident, by his own admission he had just finished texting."

Loomis walked midway down the jury box and stopped. "Ladies and gentlemen of the jury, Mr. Farrell was not paying full attention to his driving when he struck and killed young Vincent Degregorio. In this era of distraction by smart phone, you, the jury, have an opportunity to send a message to the world that driving is serious business. The judge will instruct you before you begin your deliberations that the standard of proof in a civil suit is a preponderance of the evidence. That is what I ask you to consider: the sum total of Mr. Farrell's inattention and distraction from his driving. If you do that, and if you place that in context with what followed – the death of a promising young man – I think you will decide for the plaintiff. I thank you for paying such close attention during these proceedings. No one is happy that this trial had to occur, but you have the opportunity to bring closure to one family's tragedy. Thank you very much."

And Loomis returned to the plaintiff's table. He walked slowly to let his words linger in the air as long as possible.

When he was seated, Judge Larson said, "Mr. Mixner, your closing statement please."

Alec stood and buttoned his jacket. He looked youthful, eager, earnest. He closed the distance to the jury box with swift steps. Every juror stared at him.

Alec cleared his throat. "This has been a difficult case to try because so much is in doubt. You won't find the accident on YouTube. The eyewitnesses who saw the accident differ on details. There is no DNA test which can prove who did what. You are being asked to determine who was paying attention and who wasn't, who looked and who didn't. You are the sole deciders of facts."

Alec stepped to within touching distance of the jury box and spread his arms, as if to say I have nothing to hide.

"You have heard the defendant testify that he texted his wife before he started to turn onto the interstate. You have heard Mr. Loomis try to make that the cause of the accident. Well, it was wrong for my client to text while driving, but if he had finished before he made his turn – as he claims – it has no relevance to this trial. There is no proof that the texting led to the accident that resulted in Mr. Degregorio's death. None."

Alec prowled to the end of the jury box.

"Now we come to the heart of this case. What was Vincent Degregorio, Jr. doing before the accident? You heard testimony that he was traveling at a high rate of speed on his bicycle. You heard the defendant say that Mr. Degregorio passed him on the right at a stoplight, then fell behind after the light turned green. Was Mr. Degregorio paying attention to the other traffic on the road? Was he paying attention when Mr. Farrell begin his turn onto the Interstate? Was he trying to beat the traffic? Mr. Loomis hasn't focused on that for obvious reasons. He doesn't want you to think about it. We don't know and can never know for sure, and all of us wish to shield the deceased's family from additional pain, but the truth of the matter, ladies and gentlemen of the jury, is that the deceased may have been looking at a pretty woman across the street, or at a flock of geese, may have been wondering how the Red Sox were doing, may have been thinking about everything except the traffic surrounding him. No one knows. We do know that bicycle riders sometimes show disdain for red lights and one-way streets. How many of us, when crossing a street at a crosswalk, haven't almost been clipped by a bicyclist who has ignored the red light? We'll never know to what extent Mr. Degregorio, Jr. was to blame, we'll never know to what extent Mr. Farrell was to blame, and we'll never know to what extent this was a tragic, unavoidable accident, the fault of neither man. Proof is lacking, and that, ladies and gentlemen of the jury, means placing blame on one or the other is no fairer than deciding the case by flipping a coin."

Alec surveyed the impassive faces of the jury. "Before you begin your deliberations, Judge Larson will instruct you on the law, and I guarantee you that one thing he won't tell you to do is flip a coin to reach your verdict. A life has been lost. Don't compound the tragedy by flipping a coin. Thank you for your close attention throughout this trial."

As if a switch had been thrown, everyone in the courtroom – litigants, jurors, and spectators – stirred at once. Judge Larson banged his gavel. He waited until the courtroom quieted, then read the jury its instructions.

"Let's go get coffee," Alec suggested when the judge finished.

Ernie asked, "How long will it take the jury to decide?"

Alec deferred to Jim, who answered, "No way to predict. I had juries reach a verdict almost before I could get to chambers, and I had juries take days and days."

"What do you think the verdict will be?"

"Don't guess. Wait and see. The wait is the hardest part of a trial. Alec, you did a fine job. Well done."

There was no verdict by the end of the day. Judge Larson summoned the parties to the courtroom to dismiss the jury for the night. "Be here at the usual time tomorrow morning and resume your deliberations. In the meantime, remember you are not to discuss the case with anyone, including spouses or other members of the jury."

The jury signaled they had a verdict just before noon the next day.

Jim didn't subscribe to the myth that one can predict verdicts by whether jurors look at the defendant on their way into the courtroom. Some jurors stare blatantly at the defendant, liberated from the need to remain detached; some jurors stare straight ahead, as if dreading what is to come. You can't tell verdicts from faces.

When the jurors were all in their places, Judge Larson asked, "Has the jury reached a verdict?"

"Yes, Your Honor," the foreman answered.

"The defendant will rise. Ladies and gentlemen of the jury, what is your verdict?"

"In the case of Degregorio v. Farrell, we find for the plaintiff, Vincent Degregorio."

A sigh, a gasp throughout the courtroom. The judge gaveled for silence.

"And what is your recommendation for sentence?"

"The jury recommends that the defendant compensate the plaintiff for the funeral and burial expenses of Vincent Degregorio, Jr., and pay damages in the amount of $1."

Pandemonium broke out. "Silence, silence," Judge Larson gaveled. "So say you all?"

One by one, the jurors affirmed their verdict.

"Thank you, ladies and gentlemen. Mr. Farrell, please make arrangements for payment at the clerk's office on your way out. Court is adjourned."

And like that it was done.

Vincent Degregorio left the courtroom hurriedly without a word, trailed by his lawyers. Janet and Ernie hugged for a long moment. Alec collected his papers. Jim waited until everyone had gone. He wanted no part of the circus that would flare as a result of the wrist slap, and deeper than that, he wanted no further part of grief and vindictiveness. He would carve out a life for himself that didn't involve tension, where lives didn't hang in the balance. Perhaps a life of writing and reflection in Vermont. A quiet life.

He wanted to tell Pat Knowles what had happened. Pat's court was in session but she would be breaking for lunch soon. He stopped by her courtroom and sat in the back.

She spotted him when she rose to leave the courtroom. With a nod of her head, she told him to join her in chambers.

"Is your trial over?" Pat asked, hanging up her robe.

"Yes. The jury found for the plaintiff and fined Ernie $1. I think the jury wanted to send a message about texting while driving without financially rewarding Degregorio."

"How do you feel?"

"Spent. In need of a little R&R. How does a weekend in Vermont sound?"

15

Jim navigated the twisting streets of Beacon Hill. As a historic area, one of the oldest parts of Boston, the streets were made for carriages, not cars. The Friday afternoon traffic was brutal. Pat emerged from the door of her apartment building when Jim pulled up.

He reached across the car and opened the passenger door. "Greetings."

"Greetings, yourself."

"Ready for adventure?"

Pat climbed in. "Thrills and chills."

"I'm glad you said yes. I'm looking forward to this."

"So am I. How do you feel now that the trial is over?"

"Relieved. Wondering why I felt compelled to represent Ernie Farrell. I saw something in him that I thought was worth saving, that's part of it, but there is more. I like the law, perhaps more than I realized. Maybe over the weekend I'll fully understand what that means for my retirement."

The former factory towns along Route 2 in central Mass looked hollow and abandoned. Pat looked country-ready in the car. This was only the second time Jim had seen her in jeans and it was still a jolt.

"I'm done with courtrooms," Jim said as he drove. "I thought maybe I'd want to try other cases, but never again. My nerves can't take it."

"Never say never."

They reached the Vermont border in good time. Sun streaked the hillsides. "Ernie matured a lot during the trial. He'll be fine now."

"Did his father ever come to the trial?"

"Never. Neither the criminal nor the civil trial."

Pat looked out the passenger window. "I don't understand how a parent can reject a child. It's beyond me."

"I think Ernie can cope now. Janet I'm a little more worried about."

The hills of Vermont had rarely looked so good. When they reached the narrow street that climbed to his house, Jim slowed. His house faced east just below the top of the ridge. A good vantage point for sunrise walks. Jim felt an overpowering sense of relief as he unlocked his front door.

"Come in," he said to Pat. "Welcome to my hideaway once again."

The smell of stale air leapt up to greet them when Jim opened the door. He hung up their coats and joined her in the living room. "Something to drink?"

"Water would be good."

Jim poured some from the refrigerator. He carried it to the long windows in the living room where Pat was standing and handed it to her. "Well water. Filtered."

She took it and drank. "It's good to be back. Do you ever tire of this view?"

"Never."

They bought food at the general store and ate dinner at the house. Jim's thoughts wandered pleasantly as Pat watched dusk settle over the valley. He felt new. Ernie's two trials had ended and Jim was still in one piece. Technically he was missing a piece, but he was healthy, and Pat was here, at his place. "At the risk of bringing fate down on my head, I think I'm happy."

"Don't be reckless."

"You're right. I shouldn't jump to conclusions."

"Until you know all the facts."

"Until I've considered all the evidence."

He raised his glass. "Here's to two judges, one a pushover, the other as strong as they come."

"Which is which?" She reached across the table to click glasses. They drank. "I like this wine. Is it expensive?"

"Not at all. $12. If you spend more for wine, you're showing off."

"Aren't you showing off by saying that?"

"I think I need a lawyer."

"What shall we do tomorrow?" she asked. Her eyes, her voice, implied a smile but her face remained expressionless.

"I'll show you some valleys I especially like," he replied. Jim had a sudden premonition that something bad was going to happen tomorrow. He was not a man given to premonitions. He had no idea why he had one now. Why couldn't he relax and enjoy Pat's company?

Pat slept in the guest bedroom across the hall from Jim's. In his bedroom, Jim fought sleep. Closure of one chapter, the start of another. He wanted to be awake to mark the passage.

He drove to the general store in the morning before Pat was awake and returned with newspapers and sugar donuts. Pat was up by the time he returned. When he opened the brown paper bag and showed her the donuts, she was appalled. He pleaded his case, "My cholesterol's good."

"Not for long."

"I only eat these here."

"You're here a lot, aren't you?"

"Try 'em. They're good."

She took one. She brightened after a bite. "I knew you'd be a bad influence."

"Told you so."

She finished the doughnut and brushed sugar off her fingertips. "That was an unusually good doughnut. You know what I was thinking as I drifted off to sleep last night?"

"What were you thinking?"

"When I retire, I would like to write a book about what it's like to be a trial judge. Tedium punctuated by terror. The memoir of a trial judge. We could write it together."

"I see a major motion picture."

"I'm serious. It gives me a project to look forward to."

"So you're serious about retirement?"

"You couldn't tell?"

"Pat, you don't tip your hand. You could be plotting to kill me now and I'd never know."

Her expression didn't change.

The sun, at breakfast, skipped over the river valley like a stone. Jim saw the scene through new eyes with Pat there. "Light changes everything," he commented while she gazed out the window.

"Who was it who said you can't step into the same stream twice?"

"Heraclitus."

"And Pat Knowles says you can't see the same view twice." Then Pat said, with a gravity he had never heard before, "It's beautiful up here, Jim. Simply beautiful."

In the car, after breakfast, Jim said. "I won't tell you what we're going to see until we see it." He wanted to show her the hidden hills and sudden valleys. His favorite places. He avoided anything that resembled a major road. North, then west away from the river. At one point they found themselves on a dirt road that climbed until it dead-ended in a high, dense forest. As far as Jim could tell, the road never had a destination other than the woods. "Maybe it was a logging road."

"Or maybe a second-home owner intended to build up here and chickened out."

"It's not going to be easy to turn the car around."

"I have confidence in you," Pat said.

"Want to neck a little first?"

She laughed as loudly as he had ever heard her laugh. "Sure, why not?"

After a few minutes of teenage groping, he stopped what he was doing. "I can't concentrate if you keep laughing."

"Not bad. A little overeager, but shows promise."

"I'm out of practice. Give me time."

Their pleasure was interrupted by the mini-sonic boom of a rifle echoing through the forest.

On alert, Jim asked, "Is it hunting season?" He listened intently. There it was again, a loud pop, then a lingering ping.

"It sounds far away," Pat said.

"I'm not taking any chances." He backed into the underbrush. His wheels spun, eliciting a loud, "crap!" from Jim. Then he gained traction, and with three more back-and-fills, managed a U-turn.

Another echoing ping, then pop, pop, pop.

"It's not near, Jim. It's okay."

"My missing fingertip is tingling." He gripped the steering wheel. "You're right. The shots are far away. I hate myself when I'm afraid for no reason." They made it down the mountain shaken by the rutted road.

The front door was unlocked when they got to the house.

"That's strange. I must have forgotten to lock the door. Did you notice?"

"I wasn't paying attention."

"That's not like me."

They entered and turned on the light. "I'm going to use the bathroom," Pat said.

Jim went into the living room. Although the sun was low, there was enough light to see and what Jim saw was a man sitting at the table by the long window. A scruffy-looking man with close-set eyes and a locked-in stare. Jim had seen the man before but couldn't remember the circumstances.

"Who are you and what are you doing in my living room?"

The man stood. He appeared to be about the same age as Jim, shorter by a couple of inches, roughhewn with the body of a truck driver gone to seed, eyes so close together that the bridge of his nose seemed merely a speed bump.

"I'm surprised you don't recognize me, Judge. You saw me at Ernie Farrell's trial. I sat in the back of the courtroom. You don't remember now?" The man's voice was as rough as his face.

"I do remember. I fleetingly wondered why anyone sat in the back when the courtroom was almost empty. I had no idea who you were and have no idea now. Who in hell are you?" Jim demanded, more angry than scared.

Before the intruder answered, Pat entered. She seemed startled to see another person in the house. "I didn't know we had company," she said.

"Nor did I." Jim gestured to the man. "I am now trying to determine who our visitor is. You were about to tell me, sir?"

"Does the name Roland Hawkins ring a bell?"

"No, it doesn't. And I'm tired of this game." Jim pulled his phone out of his pocket.

The man pulled a gun out of his. "Put it away, Judge. Roland Hawkins, second degree murder. Twenty-five to life. Do you remember now?"

"No, I don't. I tried hundreds of cases in my years on the bench."

The man's face lost some of its toughness. "I'm hurt, truly. I thought I had made more of an impression. Well, I had plenty of time in my cell to remember you." He seemed to notice Pat for the first time. "Who is this?" He gestured with the gun.

"Put the gun away," Jim ordered.

"Or what, Judge? You are without your gavel. Now, if you had your gavel, that would be another story." Hawkins laughed like a child, crescendoing in giggles that made his eyes water. "So, Your Honor, the gun remains. But I'll fill in the blanks for you since your memory is failing. Three men robbed a Shawmut bank in South Boston, one of the tellers got himself killed, and I took the rap, twenty-five to life. The other two ratted on me and did ten years." He paused. "You were the judge. Remember now?"

Jim did. A messy case. A plea bargain hastily arranged by the ADA and Hawkins's lawyer. Jim had not been entirely comfortable with the plea bargain. Hawkins's partners in crime were out to save their skins and were even less credible than Hawkins. But Jim as a newly appointed judge was unsure of himself, the ADA was an old hand (not Ted Conover), so Jim kept his misgivings to himself. The name Roland Hawkins still didn't ring a bell, but the trial did.

"You've changed."

Hawkins face lit up. "You remember! Good. So now you can start thinking about where I've spent the last twenty-five years." He gestured with the gun barrel at Pat. "You didn't answer my question, who's this?"

"A friend. None of your business who she is."

Hawkins eyed Pat. "I could go for her. A little old for me, but I'm no spring chicken myself." Again, the childish giggle. A man-child. Prison does that to a man, Jim thought, hardens his outsides while stunting his emotional growth.

"What do you want?" Jim demanded. "You broke in here wanting something."

"Now, that's the first correction, I didn't break in. You didn't do a very good job of hiding the spare key. You'd think a judge would be smarter than that, law degree and all."

Jim's anger at the intrusion and his fear for Pat cleansed his mind of personal fear, and he began to connect the dots. "I repeat, what do you want?"

In an instant, Hawkins changed from man-child to hardened ex-con. He gestured with the gun. "Sit on the sofa, the two of you. Side-by-side. Where I can keep an eye on you." When they did, he sat at the table by the windows. "What do I want? To see you dead."

"I'm beginning to understand." Jim held up his left hand so Hawkins could see his missing fingertip. "You're the guy who sent me a little surprise. You're the guy who did this."

"Not so dumb after all."

"How long have you been stalking me?"

"Stalking? I don't like that word. Roland Hawkins doesn't stalk. Is that what I'm doing now, stalking? I don't think so. Here to make you pay for what you did to me, is how I'd put it." Hawkins suddenly gestured to Pat. "I know you! You were the judge in the Ernie Farrell trial for vehicular homicide. I was among the spectators. You're good. I didn't recognize you without your robe."

Jim interjected. "Look, you hold the gun, which means you can kill me if that's your intent, but Judge Knowles had nothing to do with what happened to you. Let her go."

"Not possible, Judge. She's your buddy, your partner-in-crime."

"If you bear a grudge because you imagine me gloating about putting you away, let me disabuse you of the notion.

After hundreds of cases and many sleepless nights worrying whether I did the right thing in a particular case I keep my gloating to a minimum."

"You express yourself so well. No, the main reason I bear a grudge, as you put it, is because you stole my life."

"You plea bargained."

"I was confused, scared, my buddies ratted on me, and I listened to my stupid lawyer. You were the judge. You could have refused the plea."

"You're passing the buck, Hawkins." Jim shifted his weight to keep his foot from falling asleep.

"Don't you move, don't you fuckin' move!" Hawkins waved the gun.

The light hovering over the valley was fading. It felt so normal to be watching the waning of daylight through his window that Jim had a hard time accepting that an ex-con was holding a gun on them.

Hawkins laid the gun on the table beside him. Grabbing the gun was out of the question. Even if Jim were young, he couldn't reach the gun before Hawkins did.

Jim glanced at Pat as if to say, 'are you doing okay?' She caught his glance and with a quick tightening of her lips indicated she was.

"Your move," Jim said to Hawkins.

"We sit, like I sat in my prison cell. I want you to have time to think about what's going to happen to you. I want you to imagine my gun at your temple. I want you to image my finger itching to pull the trigger. I want you to be so terrified you beg me to put you out of your misery."

"How likely do you think that is?"

Hawkins airily gestured. "Oh, I don't expect to get everything I want. I'm willing to settle for seeing you piss your pants."

Jim couldn't get a fix on Hawkins. Sometimes he seemed like a delighted child pulling wings off flies, other times like a shrewd, hardened ex-con. Giddy until deadly. How can I reach him? How can I tap whatever humanity is left in him? Out loud: "Just asking, what do you plan to do with Pat?"

"As I said, I didn't expect you to have company. We'll see. I wish her no harm."

"Why don't you let her go now?"

"Oh, come on, Judge. Give me credit. If she leaves now, she'll call the cops, and the pace of events will be out of my control. No, I'm going to enjoy this, every last minute of it."

"You're holding an ex-judge and a sitting judge hostage. Unless you make some sort of deal, you'll be shot or returned to prison for life. Those are your only options. You're an intelligent man, you know there is no escape."

Hawkins shook his head. "So what? What kind of life do I have? None. No one will hire me. Look at me, I'm not a ladies' man, so women are out of the question. What do I have to live for?"

He had given Jim an opening. "Don't you have kids? I seem to remember you did."

"Good man, it's starting to come back to you. Yes, I have kids. Sheila divorced me while I was in prison, married a prison guard she met when she visited me – can you imagine the crazy things people do? And my kids, I have no idea where they are. They're ashamed of their dad is my guess. Can't blame them."

"If I were in your shoes, I'd want to find out if they hold a grudge against their father. Maybe you're imagining their reactions all wrong. Maybe they'd welcome you reaching out."

"Theoretically possible, but it's too late for that."

"No, it's not. Turn yourself in and I'll make sure you get to see your kids."

"If they're alive. If they want to see me."

"How many do you have?"

"Three. Molly, who would be forty-two, George, thirty-eight, and Mikey, thirty-six."

"You remember their ages. Good for you. Not all dads do, especially when they've been out of touch. Do you have grandkids?"

Hawkins lowered his eyes and nodded.

"How many?"

"The last I heard, three."

"If you die, they'll never know their grandfather. They'll never know that you regret what you did. Reunite with your children and grandchildren, get to know them, seek their forgiveness for not being there when they were growing up. Make amends, take responsibility."

"That's where you go off the rails, right there." Hawkins stabbed the air with his finger. "It's your fault I wasn't there for them, not mine. If you hadn't accepted the plea bargain, I'd be a free man long ago. You should ask them for forgiveness, not me."

From what Jim could remember, Hawkins was an accomplice, a hanger-on, the kind of crook other crooks took advantage of. A man who was a puppet but thought he was the puppeteer.

"I need to use the bathroom," Jim said, to gain himself a moment to think.

"Before you do, your cellphone, please. And yours too," Hawkins said to Pat. "Oh, in case you're wondering, I cut your landline before I came in, and I checked, there are no neighbors close enough to hear shouting, so don't bother."

Jim handed over his phone. As he did, the phone rang.

"How do you turn this damn thing off?" Hawkins said.

"I'll show you." Jim set the phone to vibrate. Before he handed it over, he glanced at who called: Ernie Farrell. "Now may I use the bathroom?"

"Number one or number two?" Hawkins deadpanned, followed by the giggles. Give him a reason to giggle and Hawkins was a happy man. He waved his hand. "Go. Do your business. But keep the door open. Judge Knowles and I will be just outside the door."

The bathroom was off the kitchen. Jim tried but couldn't pee.

"What's taking you so long?" Hawkins called after a few moments.

Jim raised his voice. "I don't know about you, but my prostate delights in reminding me who is boss."

Hawkins appeared at the door. He had his arm around Pat's neck and the gun to her head. "Really? You have prostate trouble too?"

Jim scowled over his shoulder. "Would you mind?"

"Sorry." Hawkins jerked his head aside. He sounded embarrassed.

His embarrassment confirmed for Jim that Hawkins was a man-child, albeit one with a malicious streak and a gun. Unpredictable. Explosive. Not a hardened criminal, but dangerous for all that.

As he stood at the toilet, Jim's summers on Lake Winnipesaukee as a boy came to mind. The mental picture of blue skies over rippling water apparently pleased his prostate and allowed him to pee. That's one small step for a hostage, one giant step for my prostate, Jim said to himself. He flushed the toilet.

Hawkins hovered in the hallway. "All done? Good man. Do you need to go?" he asked Pat.

"No."

"Either of you two hungry?"

"As a matter of fact," Jim answered. He wasn't, but eating might distract Hawkins. "But there isn't much in the refrigerator."

"Way ahead of you. I went grocery shopping before I came. A few of my favorite foods." He removed a paper bag from the refrigerator and put it on the counter. "I thought of everything. Okay, one at a time, step up and help yourself."

Jim looked at Pat. "You first." He leaned close and whispered. "We'll be okay."

She nodded.

"What are you two whispering about?"

"Planning our escape."

"Ha, ha. That's a good one. Okay, who's going first?"

Jim stepped to the counter and looked in the bag: ham, cheese, a loaf of local bread, and a liter of diet Pepsi. "You're missing a few food groups."

Hawkins ignored Jim's wisecrack. He slapped his forehead. "You know what I forgot? Mustard! You got any mustard?"

"I think so. Check the fridge."

Hawkins did as he was told. Jim committed to memory: childlike *and* compliant. Bide your time.

They ate in the living room. Never had Jim enjoyed food less. From the look on Pat's face, she felt the same. Hawkins, on the other hand, relished each morsel, grinning as he wiped mustard off his lips. "You got good bread up here."

Jim adopted a judicial tone. "I have a question for you, Hawkins. Don't hostage takers read demands in front of TV cameras? The hostage situations I've known have always involved demands and negotiations, often public."

"Not this one. No demands or negotiations this time."

"So no one is going to know that you've gotten revenge for the life that was stolen from you?"

"You'll know."

"What good is that? Don't you want others to know how you outwitted the judge who put you away? How you made him suffer? When you kill me without explanation or demands, you'll just seem like a loser."

"But you'll be dead. That makes me a winner."

"In your own eyes, no one else's."

"Bullshit! Enough talk, Judge. You're giving me a headache." Hawkins rubbed his temples.

Jim replied, "I'll shut up, but think about your legacy. Don't you want your kids to remember you with at least some pride? Don't die in shame, tell your story to the world. Think, Hawkins. Think."

The menace returned to Hawkins's eyes. "I ought to kill you now. You got me into this mess. You put me into this dilemma." Hawkins stopped rubbing his temples, his little boy look replaced by the glare of a jail-hardened killer.

Jim felt calm. Maybe – he thought – this is what extreme panic feels like.

"It's too soon to put you out of your misery," Hawkins concluded. "I'm going to make you pay for what you did. Settle in, you two. I want you to have plenty of time to think about your fate."

Pat spoke for the first time. "Mr. Hawkins, you miscalculated."

"What do you mean?"

"Did you know I'd be here? Did you plan for a sitting judge to be in the picture?"

"No, not really."

"I complicate things. If I don't show up for work, the police will come looking for me. The solution is as Judge Randall suggests, call the police and negotiate a deal. If you're as smart as you think you are, you can come out of this looking like a man who took revenge on the judge who put you away, and who was smart enough to come out of it alive when events didn't turn out as planned. An ex-con who held the authorities to a standoff long enough to make a deal. A hero in the eyes of those who wish they could outsmart the authorities. Think how that will feel. Most men never get to be a hero in the eyes of others even for a second."

Hawkins scoffed. "You don't understand, my motive is revenge against Judge Randall, period, I'm not out for glory. Besides, no way in hell will the cops indulge me long enough to make a deal."

Jim was tired of this man-child. "You never know until you try."

"Enough. Settle in. The three of us will spend the night together here in your country home where you go to escape your everyday troubles." Hawkins found that hysterically funny. He couldn't stop laughing. He laughed and laughed.

16

Sleep was out of the question. Jim and Pat sat side-by-side on the sofa. Hawkins sat at the long table by the windows. A crescent moon crossed the sky. Finally Hawkins could stay awake no longer and hogtied Jim and Pat back-to-back on the floor by the sofa, then looped one end of the rope tightly around his wrist and stretched out on the sofa. "You learn to sleep lightly in prison. I warn you, don't try anything. I can feel every twitch you make."

Hawkins snored while he slept. On the floor below him, Jim whispered to Pat, "I'm so sorry I got you involved in this."

"I guess hogtied back-to-back constitutes a new definition of sleeping together," Pat said. "I doubt it will catch on. Who was that who called you?"

"Ernie Farrell."

"Will he worry when you don't call back?"

"Why should he?"

"When I don't show up in court, my colleagues will worry," Pat said.

"But how will they find you? Does anyone know you're up here?"

She thought for a minute. "No, I didn't tell anyone."

Hawkins awoke with a start at the first light of dawn. His sudden movement tightened the rope tying him to Jim and Pat.

"Ouch!" Pat cried.

"Careful, dammit," Jim said.

"Sorry." Hawkins sounded contrite. He untied Pat and Jim. "Don't do anything stupid. Remember I've got a gun."

Neither Pat nor Jim could stand at first. Slowly and with considerable pain, feeling returned to their limbs, and they helped one another to their feet.

"Hungry?" Hawkins asked as if it was just another morning.

Jim looked at Pat. "I guess we could eat something."

"I bought eggs yesterday at the store. I like my eggs over easy. Either of you cook?"

"What's the matter? You can't?"

"Prison cells don't come with kitchens."

"I'll cook," Pat said, rubbing the circulation into her forearms and hands.

"No, let me," Jim said. "Eggs are the only thing I can cook."

Hawkins stood guard while Jim cooked. "Smells good," he said.

When the eggs were ready, Hawkins ate his standing up. "This exceeds my wildest expectations."

"Thank you," Jim said.

"I don't mean the eggs, I mean that you cooked them. Imagine. In all the years rotting in my cell, I never dreamed the judge who put me there would one day cook me eggs." He laughed bitterly. "Life is full of unexpected twists and turns, isn't it?" He laughed until his throat turned dry.

Jim put the frying pan in the sink and turned on the water. "By the time you get around to killing me, I'm going to seem so ordinary as to not be worth it." He raised his voice so Hawkins could hear him over the sound of the water hitting the hot skillet. "You're going to view me as just another working stiff who did his job as best he could. So you better hurry up before you lose your drive. Finish your eggs and let's get it over with."

"Jim, what are you doing?" Pat sounded alarmed.

"He's not going to do anything rash. He's got this planned. Right, Hawkins?"

Hawkins looked a little befuddled. "Yeah, that's right. According to plan." He nodded his head as if to reassure himself.

Jim carried his plate past Hawkins to the livingroom.

"Where are you going?" Hawkins asked.

"Where do you think? To the table."

"No, you don't." Hawkins pointed the gun barrel at the sofa. "You and your sweetheart will eat there on the sofa, side-by-side, so I can keep an eye on you. I'm not wrong about you two, am I?"

"Yes, you are. We're just friends."

Hawkins sat down at the table with his plate. "You can't fool me. I've seen the way you look at each other. Like two people who know each other carnally." Again Hawkins started laughing. Again he couldn't stop. "Carnally! I like that."

"You have a way with words," Jim said.

Hawkins's laughter abruptly died. "Don't mock me! Don't you dare mock me!"

"For a tough guy you have very thin skin."

Hawkins's mood shifted. "I read a lot of philosophy in prison, I'm a learned man. My mother wanted me to go to college but I never did. It might surprise you who my favorite philosophers are. Try to guess."

"I give up."

Hawkins almost beamed. "The Stoics. Don't sweat the small stuff."

"A good philosophy."

Hawkins paused to think. "I still haven't decided what to do with Judge Knowles. She didn't have anything to do with sending me away. But she's with you. See what I mean? Fess up, Judge, you two are lovers. How is she in bed?"

Jim swallowed his disgust. "You're an asshole, Hawkins."

"Yes, but how is she? I mean, between us guys."

Stay cool, Jim; he's baiting you. "You tell me you're smart then act like the crudest sort of thug. Get it over with, take your cheap revenge on me but let Pat go. She had nothing to do with your going to prison, and for your information, we're not sleeping together."

"It's only a matter of time, Judge. A matter of time. Stand up."

Hawkins approached the sofa and thrust the gun barrel in Jim's mouth.

Pat screamed.

Hawkins withdrew the gun and winked at Pat. "Thought I'd do it, didn't you? Had you scared, didn't I? Damn, I love this!"

Jim surprised himself by remaining calm even when the gun was in his mouth. If he survived maybe he'd fall to pieces, but for now he felt like an observer, not a hostage.

"Hawkins, what did you dream of being when you were a kid? I'll bet it wasn't this."

Hawkins returned to the table and squinted out the window at the sun. "I didn't do much dreaming, I didn't have that luxury. That's something you wouldn't understand. I never knew my dad. I'm not even sure my mom knew who my father was. Mom's boyfriend moved in with us when I was twelve. He stayed home while my mom worked two jobs. He is the only man I hate more than you."

"Did he beat you?"

Hawkins looked at Jim as if he were the dumbest man who ever lived. "Of course he beat me! What do you think?"

"How should I know?"

"He routinely beat the shit out of me. It was as routine as getting dressed in the morning."

"Help me remember. When were you first arrested?"

"At age fourteen."

"For what?"

A touch of pride entered Hawkins's voice. "I beat a kid half to death with a baseball bat."

"It's coming back to me. You spent your teens in a juvenile facility. That must have been hard on you."

"It got me away from home. I only got beat up once in a while."

"You've spent more time incarcerated than free, if I remember correctly."

Again, the flash of pride. "You do, yes."

"You must have hated that."

"It gets to be comfortable. The days have rules and routines. If I could live my life over, I'd become a lawyer. I'd be spectacular."

Jim nodded. "I think you'd be good. You're a lot more intelligent than people give you credit for. People judge others by their exteriors, not by who they are inside. But I've gotten to know you. You've got a lot going on inside you. Life hasn't worked out for you, but you're not a bad person. I know that and you know that."

Hawkins turned and looked out the window. Mist was rising from the valley, reminding Jim of steam from the espresso machines at The Long Gone. "One thing I missed in prison was windows. You don't know how important windows are until you don't have any." Hawkins turned back to the table. He picked up his fork and took the last bite of eggs. "The other thing I missed was good food. The food inside stinks. First thing I did when I got out was eat a cheeseburger and a giant order of onion rings at the greasiest spoon I could find. Puked for a day and night. Loved every minute."

"That's New Hampshire out the window, did you know that?" Jim said to keep Hawkins distracted.

Hawkins turned in surprise. "Where? I don't see it."

"Yes, you do, you're looking at it. Can you make out the river? It's hard to see because of the glare, but everything you see on the other side of the river is New Hampshire."

"No, shit? New Hampshire, huh? From this angle it looks like New Jersey." Hawkins turned away from the window. "I'm wrong, what was I thinking? Jersey has those huge gasoline storage tanks and the foulest smelling air in the world. I hate New Jersey."

"Have you done time there?"

Hawkins answered, "No, but I've driven through it on the Turnpike." Hawkins had reached a pause, a timeout. He seemed unsure what to do next. He pulled Jim's cellphone out of his pocket and studied it.

"What are you doing?" Jim asked.

"It just vibrated. I thought you turned it off." Hawkins fumbled with the phone. "I'm not good with these."

"That's a warning the battery's running low. Here, I'll turn it off." Jim reached for the phone.

Hawkins crossed the room and handed Jim the phone. Ernie had texted him several times wondering where he was. Apparently Hawkins hadn't felt the vibrations until now, or maybe he felt them and didn't know what they were.

Jim turned off the phone and handed it back. Hawkins stuck it in his pocket and snapped his fingers. "Okay, you two. I've decided. Today is the day. I'll let you pick the time of your death. You first, Judge Randall."

Pat couldn't contain her disgust. "You're a sadist."

Hawkins laughed. "Let Judge Randall answer. What do you say?"

"I'm not going to give you the pleasure."

Hawkins spun away from the table. "Gotcha! I *love* this! I fuckin' love this!"

"You're being ridiculous," Jim said.

Hawkins's face clouded. "What did you say?"

"I said, you're being ridiculous."

Hawkins planted his face an inch from Jim's. "Shut up. Understood?"

"Hawkins, think for once in your sorry life. Our friends will worry when they don't hear from us. They'll ask the police to check on us. While you're playing the tough guy, the police may be surrounding the house."

"You're bluffing."

"Are you sure?"

Hawkins walked to the front door and peered out the window. "I don't see anybody." He came back. "I know the game you're playing. I'll tell you what. If you won't pick the time of your death, I'll pick it for you but won't tell you what it is. In fact, I'll do that now." Hawkins pressed his left palm to his forehead, like a fortune teller. "It's locked in! The time of your death! Hear the clock ticking?"

In fact, Jim did. The ticking of the kitchen clock echoed hollowly throughout the house. Nothing in Jim's contemplative life had prepared him for a life span measured by the ticking of a clock. He had meant to replace the clock long ago. Keep Hawkins talking. "It's up to you, Hawkins. You still have control. Pull that trigger and you lose it."

Hawkins ignored him. "Relax, Judge. You have a few more minutes. Tell me something. Why did you believe Simon and Ralph?"

"Who the hell are Simon and Ralph?"

"The rats who turned states' evidence against me."

"It was a long time ago. I don't remember the details of your trial."

"I'll help you out. Simon thought one of the bank tellers was reaching for the panic button and shot him. Simon was always doing things like that."

"What's your point?"

"Why did you believe them when they fingered me for the killing?"

"I repeat, you accepted a plea bargain."

"Only when my lawyer convinced me the jury would find me guilty of murder in the first degree and I'd get life without parole. When I put a bullet through your brain, you can blame it on the plea bargain." Hawkins dissolved in laughter. "The question stands, why did I end up doing twenty-five years when Simon and Ralph only did ten?"

"Weren't there eyewitnesses? Didn't one of the tellers identify you as the killer?"

"Yes, she did. But she admitted she was scared and only got a glimpse."

"A life of crime. Would you deny that's the life you led?"

"Not at all."

"And didn't you stop to think that someday it would end badly? Did you expect to enjoy a tranquil old age, maybe move to a warm climate, sip cool drinks on a beach?"

Hawkins abruptly stood. "Okay, I'm bored. Let's get it over with. Judge, lie on the floor, face down."

"What are you doing?"

"You think I've been kidding? You think I'm doing this to pass the time? Get on the floor."

Pat's eyes grew huge. Jim looked at her. "I'll do what you say, Hawkins, but you have to promise me you won't harm Pat."

Hawkins snarled, "I already told you, I got nothing against her."

Jim dropped to his knees on the floor. "You'll let her go after you kill me?"

"After I kill you, she'll be free to do as she pleases." That apparently put a thought in Hawkins's head. "Will you do something for me?" he asked Pat.

Pat sputtered in confusion. "You are about to kill the man I love and you want me to do something for *you*?"

"Yes. I'm asking you to tell the truth about me. Tell everyone I'm a wronged man, not a madman."

"I'll do nothing of the sort," Pat replied. "If you want the world to know your story, you'll have to tell it yourself. Which means call the police, negotiate the right to make a statement. Better yet, you could let me negotiate on your behalf. You don't have a grudge against me, and the police will listen to a sitting judge. I don't think you really want to die. I think you're scared of life on the outside and want to go back inside. I can help you."

Jim was awed by Pat's nerve. Hawkins seemed befuddled by her words. "Let me think. I need to think this through. Stay on the floor," he gestured with the gun when Jim shifted his weight. "And you, sit on the sofa," he said to Pat.

"No. I've been sitting a long time. I'll stand, if you don't mind. Shoot me if that bothers you so much."

"Women!" Hawkins shook his head. "Thank god I didn't serve time with women!"

Pat said, "Think, Mr. Hawkins. As long as Judge Randall remains alive, you hold the cards. Don't squander your advantage. Call the police and negotiate now."

Hawkins scowled, rubbed his forehead. "This isn't working out the way I planned. I didn't count on a woman being here."

"I agree with Judge Randall," Pat continued. "I see you as an intelligent man, a man who knows his own mind, a man who trusts his instincts. Prove me right. Trust your instincts, Mr. Hawkins."

Hawkins steadied his head. A smile spread over his face. "You almost had me there. On the sofa! And you," he gestured at Jim. "Off the floor!"

Jim looked up at him. "Off the floor? I just got here."

"Both of you. Side by side on the sofa. Two are better than one."

Someone knocked on the door. Hawkins gestured at Pat. "See who it is. But don't open it." When Pat didn't move, he hissed, "Do it!"

"Do what he says Pat," Jim urged.

Pat stood and approached the door. "It's a state trooper."

"Ask him what he wants."

Pat raised her voice so she could be heard through the door. "Is there anything wrong, officer?" The trooper's muffled reply: "I'm Trooper Wilson, ma'am. We were asked to check on Judge Randall. Is everything okay?"

"Fine, officer. I'm Judge Knowles. Thanks for checking."

"A man named Ernie Farrell asked us to check on Judge Randall's well-being. Could you open the door, please?"

"Jim's napping. I don't want to wake him. But everything's fine."

"I'd like to see for myself, ma'am."

"Hear what I'm saying. We'll be fine as long as I don't open the door."

The trooper stood for another minute, saying nothing. Pat hoped he had picked up on her call for help. He seemed to be conferring with someone on the other side of the door. His voice was brisk when he replied. "Then we'll be going. Call us if you need us."

Hawkins waited until he heard a car start. "Nicely done. Now join Judge Randall on the sofa. Nice matching wits with you two, but it's time to do the deed." His voice left no room for doubt.

Pat did as she was told. When she was seated, Hawkins held his gun against Jim's head. "No way I can kill you both with one bullet. Now *that* would be cool."

"You said you'd let Pat go," Jim said.

"I changed my mind. I don't like mouthy women."

Jim glanced at Pat with sorrow.

"Not your fault," she whispered.

Hawkins guffawed. "You lovebirds can hold hands if you want. Ready?"

An amplified voice burst through the back window. "State Troopers! The house is surrounded! Drop your weapon!"

"What the fuck?" Hawkins ducked behind the sofa, out of sight of the window.

The trooper's voice over the megaphone came wrapped in steel wool, which made it all the more commanding.

"We've got you covered. If you show your head we will take you out before you can pull your trigger. Drop your weapon now and come out with your hands up."

All of Jim's attention had been focused on where Hawkins's bullet would enter his head. Now his attention shifted to the window. He glimpsed a megaphone, rifles.

"Kill me, I don't care!" Hawkins screamed from behind the sofa.

"Who are you?" the trooper demanded.

"Roland Hawkins! Free man, ex-con, a victim of Judge Randall's kangaroo court! I'm prepared to die but he's going with me. Who are *you*?"

"Trooper Wilson, and no one's going to die unless we do the killing. We are very good shots. Come out with your hands above your head."

"Not a chance!"

"What is your purpose? What do you want?"

"What do I want? The twenty-five years of my life that Judge Randall stole from me. How's that?"

"If you feel you have been wronged, cooperate with us and we'll get your story heard. Are the judges okay?"

"Tell 'em!" Hawkins hissed

"We're fine," Jim said.

"Speak up, please, we can't hear you."

"We're fine," Jim yelled.

"Unharmed?"

"Yes, unharmed as of now. Mr. Hawkins is an intelligent man. I think he'll listen to reason."

"Good. Now let's talk about where we go from here. Mr. Hawkins, what are your demands?"

"Demands is the wrong word," Hawkins yelled. "Reparations is more like it."

"As you wish. What do you want in return for the release of the two judges?"

"I want to tell the world what it's like to rot in prison because a judge took the word of career criminals over mine."

"We can arrange for you to make a statement in front of TV cameras."

"Wait, there's more. I want to talk to the world about a court system that locks me away for twenty-five years, while the man who pulled the trigger does ten. I want to tell the world how the little guy gets screwed when judges screw up. It's not fair."

"If we promise you'll get a chance to tell your story, you'll let the judges go?"

"Not so fast. I told you I hadn't prepared a list of demands. Now that you've got me started, I have to think this through."

"We can wait. Any sign the judges' condition deteriorates, the SWAT team will be inside in a flash. When you're ready to talk seriously, call 911 and ask for me, Trooper Wilson. I'll be waiting. In the meantime, I hope you're comfortable because we're prepared for a long wait."

"Hey, listen to me! Hear me out!" Hawkins yelled.

"When you're prepared to negotiate, we can talk. In the meantime, no ad hoc agreements."

"What the fuck does that mean?"

"It means we negotiate the whole package or nothing. Call when you're ready."

Hawkins was furious. "He's gone! I didn't think this through."

"You're in charge, Hawkins. He's giving you time," Jim said.

"But I can't outlast them. There's only one of me, and they've got a shitload of troopers out there by now."

"You were prepared to die an unknown, weren't you?"

Hesitantly, "Yes."

"Then you're in a better position than before. You were going to die without anyone knowing your story. Think of this as chess, and it's your move."

"Chess. I like that. Yeah, I like that. I've got their attention, make the best of it." Behind the sofa, Hawkins got comfortable. "I'm kind of enjoying this, actually. Maybe this will be enough for me and I won't have to kill the both of you." He chuckled. "Maybe only Judge Randall."

"Take your time," Jim said. "No rush to decide."

"Come to think about it, the longer I hold out, the worse I make them look. Only problem is, I have to pee. My prostate is as ornery as yours." Hawkins thrust Jim's phone over the back of the sofa. "Here, call and tell 'em I have to take a leak. Better yet, she can call. How can they turn a woman down?"

Pat took the phone, glancing at Jim as she did. "I guess there's a first for everything." She got Trooper Wilson on the line quickly. "Mr. Hawkins has to pee." She covered the phone. "Trooper Wilson says to go on speakerphone."

"Do what he asks."

Trooper Wilson's voice was loud over the speakerphone: "Can you hear me?"

"Yes, we can," Pat said.

"You have to use the bathroom, Mr. Hawkins?"

"That's right."

"Sorry. Until you're ready to give yourself up, you're going to stay where you are. The house is surrounded. We've got men at every door and window. If you move an inch without tossing your gun out first, we will kill you. If you try to use one of the judges as a shield you'll be dead in an instant. We are superb shots. What'll it be, Mr. Hawkins?"

"Do you want me to pee my pants?"

"Speak up, Mr. Hawkins. I can't hear you."

He yelled, "Do you want me to pee my pants?"

"It is a matter of indifference to us. No bathroom breaks. Throw the gun out and give yourself up."

Trooper Wilson clicked off.

"This isn't working out the way I wanted," Hawkins groaned. "I messed up like I always do."

Pat took charge, her voice calm. "A question, Mr. Hawkins. You were respected inside, weren't you? You got out and found that things outside had changed. You don't know your way around. Weren't you more comfortable in prison than on the outside? Didn't you feel smarter and more in control in prison than out?"

"I guess I did." Hawkins sounded surprised at the thought.

"The younger guys looked up to you. You knew the ropes. You were somebody."

"That's true."

"It must have felt good, being looked up to."

"You're damn right."

"There's your answer. Outside you're nobody, inside you're somebody. Think of how much more you'll be respected now that you've held the police to a standoff and told the world your story."

Silence from Hawkins.

Jim spoke. "I'll tell you what, Hawkins. Give yourself up and I'll go to bat for you. I'm the judge who sent you away, they'll listen to me. I'll do my best to get you sent back to the same cellblock."

Pat echoed, "Think about it, Mr. Hawkins. You knew your way around in prison, you had friends, you were a role model."

Hawkins answered as if he were alone in the room, as if no one else could hear him. "Respect more than anything. I'm nobody outside. Head held high. Even though I got screwed by the system, I retain my pride."

Jim thought, how surreal. He was in the house where until yesterday he felt safer than anywhere else in the world, sitting on the sofa where he napped and read the papers, listening to an ex-con with a gun in his hand and revenge in his heart babble on about pride and prison. With a SWAT team outside ready to blow the man away. The quiet life of a retired judge.

Hawkins suddenly fell silent. Not a word. He didn't stir. Time slowed to a full stop. Jim flinched but no shots were fired.

After an interminable wait, Hawkins growled, "Give me the phone."

Jim handed Hawkins the phone.

"Roland Hawkins here. Let me speak to Trooper Wilson." A moment later, Jim heard Hawkins say, "I'm ready to deal. Yes." Pause. "No, not him." Long silence. "I have your word?" Another silence. "Okay. I'm ready."

"What now?" Jim asked Hawkins.

"She can leave."

"Say again?"

"Judge Knowles can leave."

Pat refused. "Not without Jim."

"Don't be stupid. Do what I say." Every trace of man-child had disappeared from Hawkins's voice. He sounded like the meanest son-of-a-bitch who ever lived. "Do it. *Now.*"

"Go, Pat," Jim insisted.

"No, I won't leave without you."

"Dammit, Pat! For once, don't be stubborn."

"It doesn't feel right."

"Go! Get the hell out of here!"Jim yelled, surprised to hear himself speak so harshly to someone he loved so much.

Hawkins sounded surprised. "You heard the man."

After a moment's hesitation, Pat relented. "Okay, I'm going."

"That's better. Slowly stand up. That's it." Trooper Wilson was still on the phone. "She's coming out," Hawkins said.

"Okay, we're ready for her." Over the megaphone, Wilson called, "Hands above your head, please, Judge Knowles. Now walk to the door."

Pat looked down at Jim on the sofa. "I'll see you in a bit."

Jim nodded. "Sorry to yell at you. Now get out of here."

Pat walked towards the door.

From outside: "We can see you through the window, Judge. Keep coming."

She got to the door and opened it. Jim heard a voice as Pat stepped from the house: "Are you okay, Judge Knowles? Keep your hands above your head, please."

Then silence. A silence as profound as on a Vermont winter night when the world is covered with ice. Hawkins broke the silence. "Just you and me now, Judge Randall. That's the way it should be. Just you and me."

"I'm tired of games, Hawkins. Do whatever you're going to do."

"Not quite yet."

Steady, Jim. Remember what he had intuited about Hawkins, that in spite of his mug and his gun, he had the soul of a lackey, a man-child in need of a hug. "What's the matter, Hawkins? Do you want your milk and cookies? Do you want your blankee?"

"So the esteemed judge has a breaking point. You're no better than me."

"Of course I'm no better than you, you idiot, I never said I was. But at least I'm not a psychopath."

Hawkins reacted with a wan smile. "Actually, I'm not one either, but I play one convincingly, don't you think?"

Jim caught the change in Hawkins' tone and shifted gears accordingly. "Yes, you do. Don't you want the world to know you as the intelligent man you are? Now's your chance. Give yourself up and I'll make sure you get to tell your story." Jim was surprised he sounded so calm. The unadorned voice of Jim Randall, hidden behind a judicial robe all these years. The true voice of Jim Randall.

Hawkins exhaled for what seemed like forever. "I'm tired of this, Judge. What do you say we call it a day?"

"As in, you pull the trigger?"

"As in we walk out the door and I tell my story to the world."

"You're ready to give yourself up?"

"Not give myself up, go out on top. Call the shots. How does that sound?"

"I like it."

Hawkins handed Jim the phone. "Call Trooper Wilson. Tell him we're coming. Get his promise I'll be given the chance to tell my story. And I've still got to pee. Tell him that."

Jim got Trooper Wilson on the phone. "Mr. Hawkins and I are ready to come out as long as you give him your word he'll be allowed to tell his story. And he reminds you he has to pee."

Wilson replied, "He has my word. Now both of you walk slowly to the door. Tell Hawkins to throw his gun out when he reaches the door and come out with his hands up."

Jim relayed the message to Hawkins, who nodded. "Let's go."

Jim stood. His legs were wood. No circulation, no muscle. He shuffled to the door with Hawkins behind him.

"I've enjoyed this," Hawkins said. "I liked sparring with you, Judge."

"I can't say I did."

"I understand."

At the door Hawkins called, "Here comes my gun!" Hawkins tossed the gun out. It skittered across the driveway like a child's toy.

"Step forward, hands up!"

Hawkins did as he was told.

Jim followed. On the transom Jim scanned the yard looking for Pat. He saw tons of troopers, but no Pat. "Is Judge Knowles okay?" he yelled.

A trooper emerged from behind a patrol car. Tall, dark, and handsome, what you would expect. "I'm Trooper Wilson. She's fine, Judge. She's in one of our cars. Mr. Hawkins, face down on the ground, please. Hands behind your back."

Hawkins obliged. "Remember, you promised I could pee."

"And I keep my promises." Wilson stepped forward and cuffed Hawkins's hands, then two troopers led Hawkins to a waiting police van.

Pat burst from a patrol car. "Jim!" She ran forward and embraced him. "Are you okay?"

"I'm fine."

Trooper Wilson asked, "Would you two like to go to a hospital?"

"I don't think it's necessary, do you, Pat?"

"No. Hawkins didn't hurt us." Jim felt very shaky all of a sudden. "Thank you, Trooper Wilson, and thank your fellow troopers,"

Wilson tipped his hat. "You two need time to yourselves. We'll leave you alone, but please stop by our office in the morning to give a statement." He walked to his car.

Jim put his arm around Pat. "Let's go inside."

They said little that night about their ordeal. Intelligent thought had fled, emotions were too raw. In the morning Jim and Pat told their story to Trooper Wilson and the local DA, then departed for Boston. Only then did they relax.

"You handled Hawkins beautifully," Jim said when they were on their way.

"So did you."

"It didn't feel like it. I felt totally out of control from beginning to end."

"What do you think will happen to Hawkins?" Pat said.

"I'll keep my word. I'll do what I can to get him returned to his old cell block."

"Do you think he would have killed you?"

"There's no doubt in my mind. I think he planned this meticulously. Terrorize me with a bomb, torture me by holding me hostage, then shoot me. I think he was ready to kill himself, too. What he didn't plan for was you being here. And God bless Ernie Farrell. Think of the irony: I represent Ernie in your courtroom, then he saves us by alerting the police. Full circle."

Pat stared out the car window. They were approaching Boston. "I hadn't thought of it that way, but you're absolutely right." She turned and looked at Jim. "This will make a good chapter in our memoir."

"Our memoir? News to me."

"I was going to write my memoir, but now we'll write it together."

"Can I make myself look heroic?"

"I expect no less," Pat said.

Then silence. They needed more time.

They crested the hill in Arlington and could see Boston's skyline ahead. "Do you want me to drop you at your apartment?"

"Please."

As they maneuvered the serpentine streets of Beacon Hill, he asked, "Can I come over later?"

"I want you to."

He arrived home to find his voice mail clogged with messages. He answered only one: from Ernie. Jim left a message to meet at The Long Gone next morning. Then he took a shower and a nap.

It was mid-afternoon when he called Pat. "Okay if I come over now?"

"Yes, please."

"Do you feel jet-lagged like me?"

"Jet lagged is exactly how I feel."

"I'll be there in a bit. I may walk."

"You feel that energetic?"

"No, but I need to stretch my legs and see some familiar sights to reassure myself that I really am alive, that I'm not dreaming."

Jim left his townhouse and walked through Inman Square into East Cambridge. To his relief, the chickens were still pecking in the window of the live poultry store and Beauty Shop Row was still there in all its purple splendor. Then he hit a wall. He couldn't walk another step. He hailed a cab to take him the rest of the way to Pat's.

They ate dinner at the bistro at the foot of Beacon Hill. Relief at sitting across a table from Pat in a cozy little bistro overwhelmed him. He couldn't look at her face for very long without tearing up.

After dinner, they went back to her apartment. He wanted to tell her how he felt but wasn't sure how he felt – was it love or was it relief? A near-death experience could turn emotion inside-out. He remembered something Pat had said when Hawkins was about to put a bullet through his head.

"Pat?"

"Yes, Jim?"

"When Hawkins was about to pull the trigger, he asked you to do something for him."

"I remember, and I remember I replied, how dare you ask me that when you are about to kill the man I love."

"Did you mean it, Pat? About love?"

"I meant it."

"Good, and I love you. Always have, I guess, but was too timid to admit it, even to myself. Not everyone gets a second chance to be with the one they love, Pat. Let's not waste it."

"What do you suggest?"

"I want to spend tons of time with you. I want us to be together from now on. I want to make love to you. Not in that order."

Without another word, she led him into the bedroom.

Postscript

Roland Hawkins was returned to the cell block from whence he came. Jim kept track of him at first, but eventually lost interest. By then Jim was deep into his second career as an amateur detective, assisted often by his computer guru, Ernie Farrell.

Jim and Pat are inseparable. They have never discussed the kidnaping, preferring to leave it in the past tense.